UNICORN BEING A JERK

Unicorn Being a Jerk

by

C. W. Moss

———

Books

This book is dedicated to the always incredible Mr. Steiny, the inspiringly dark Mr. Tanis, the other unicorn—Mr. Graham, the overflowing-ly joyous Kate, and the best troublemakers around, my parents.

(A blank page, for classiness.)

Hating an illustrated book.

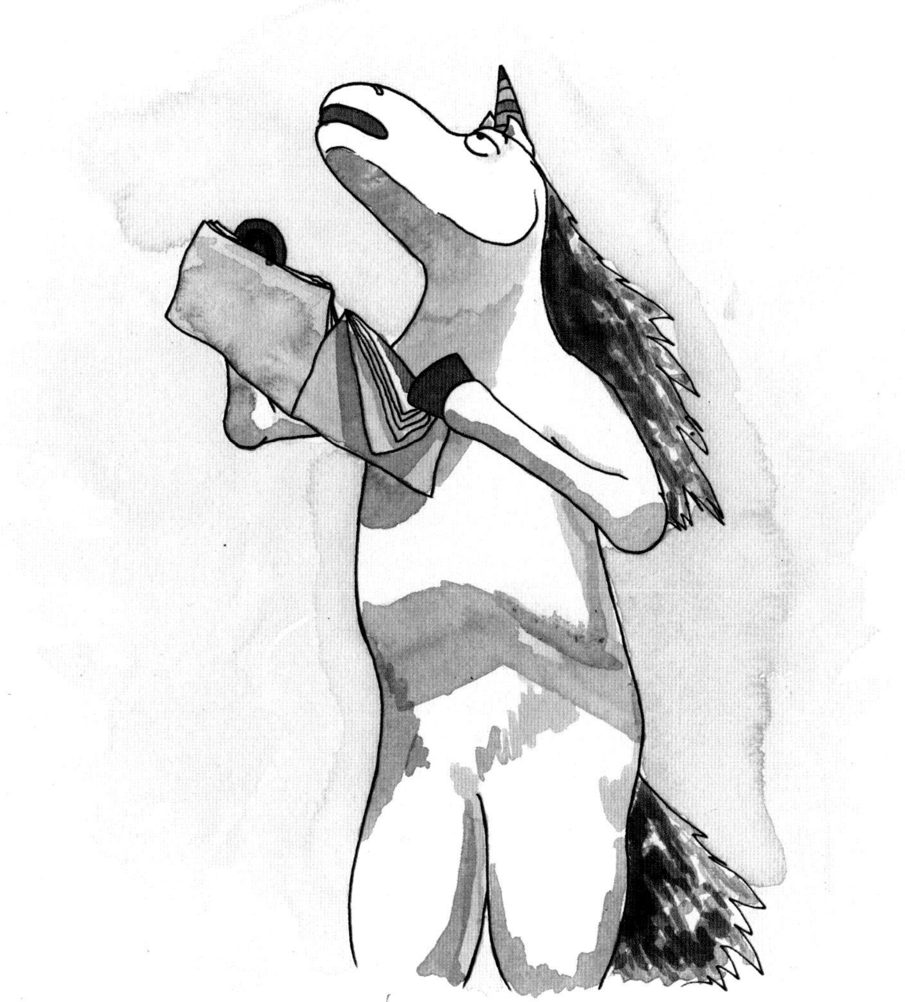

Ignoring a homeless person asking for money.

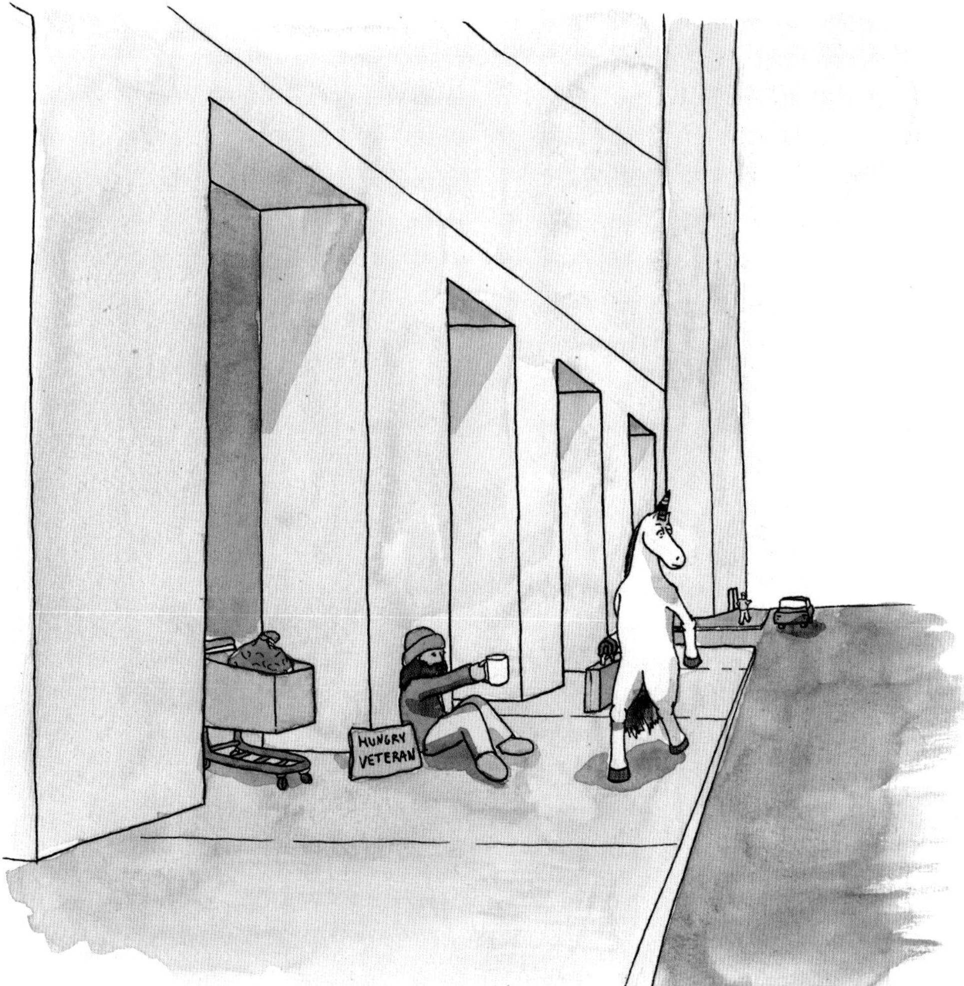
HUNGRY VETERAN

Destroying a sandcastle.

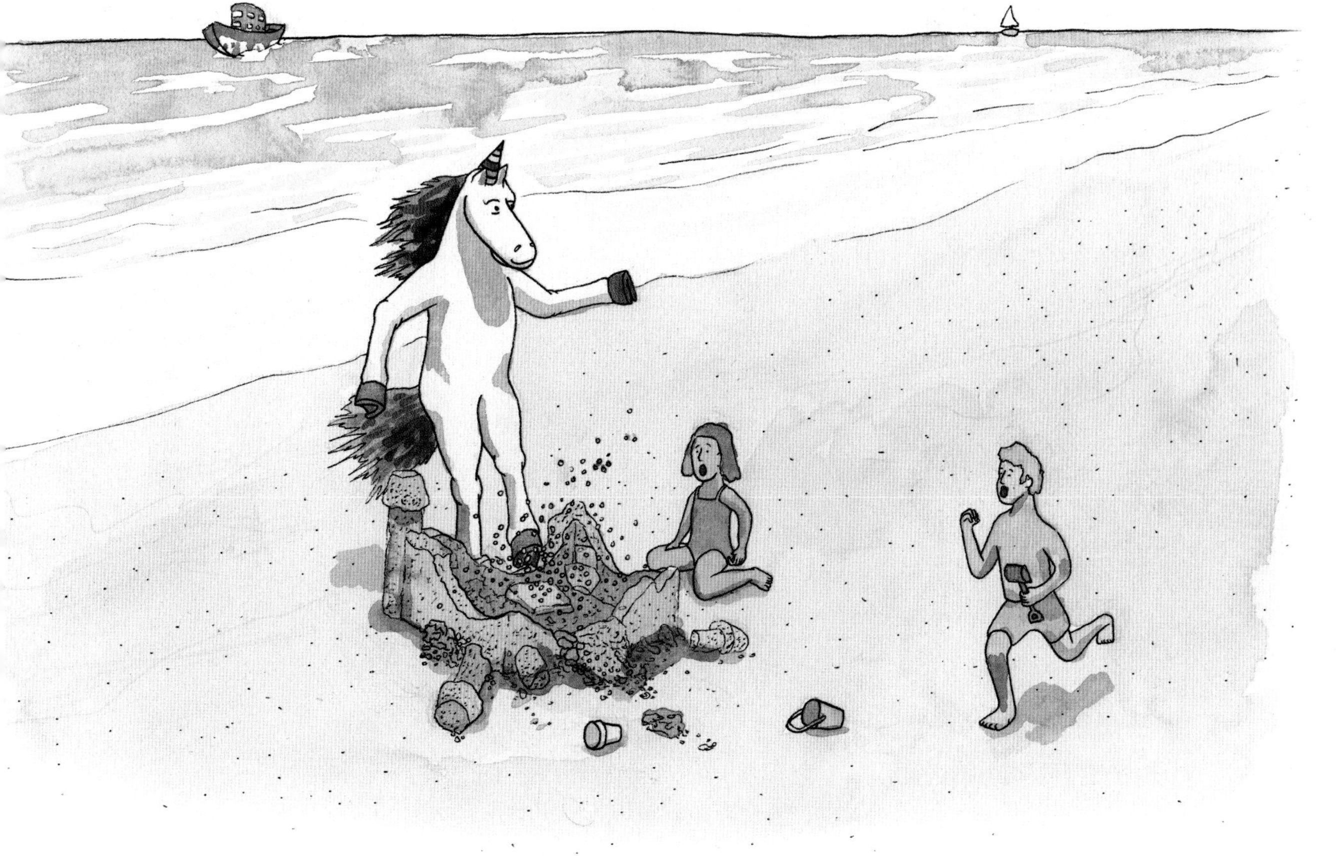

Trying to peek at a breast-feeding woman's nipple.

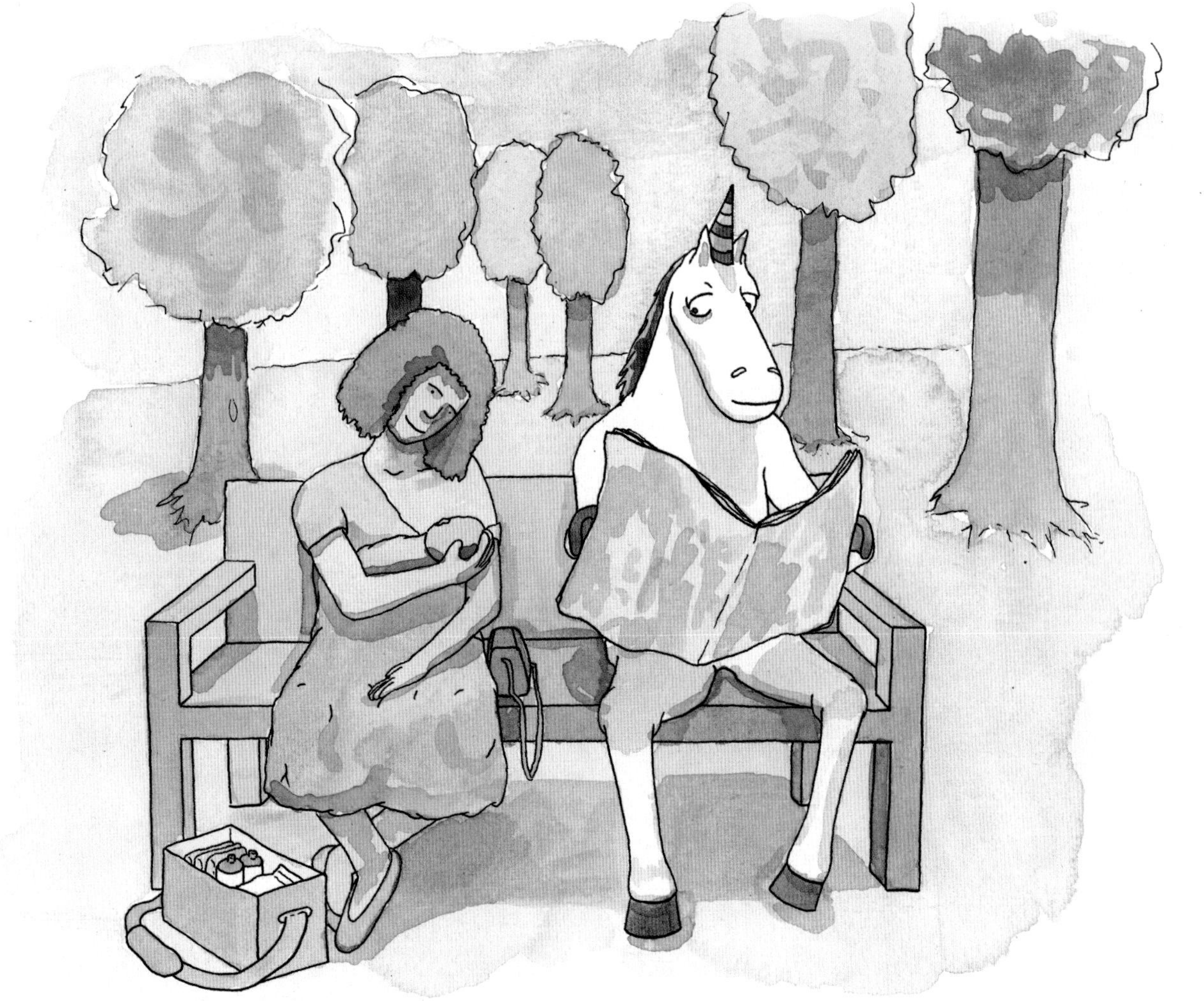

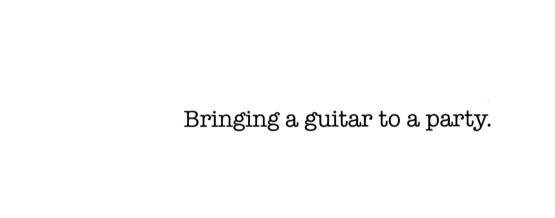

Bringing a guitar to a party.

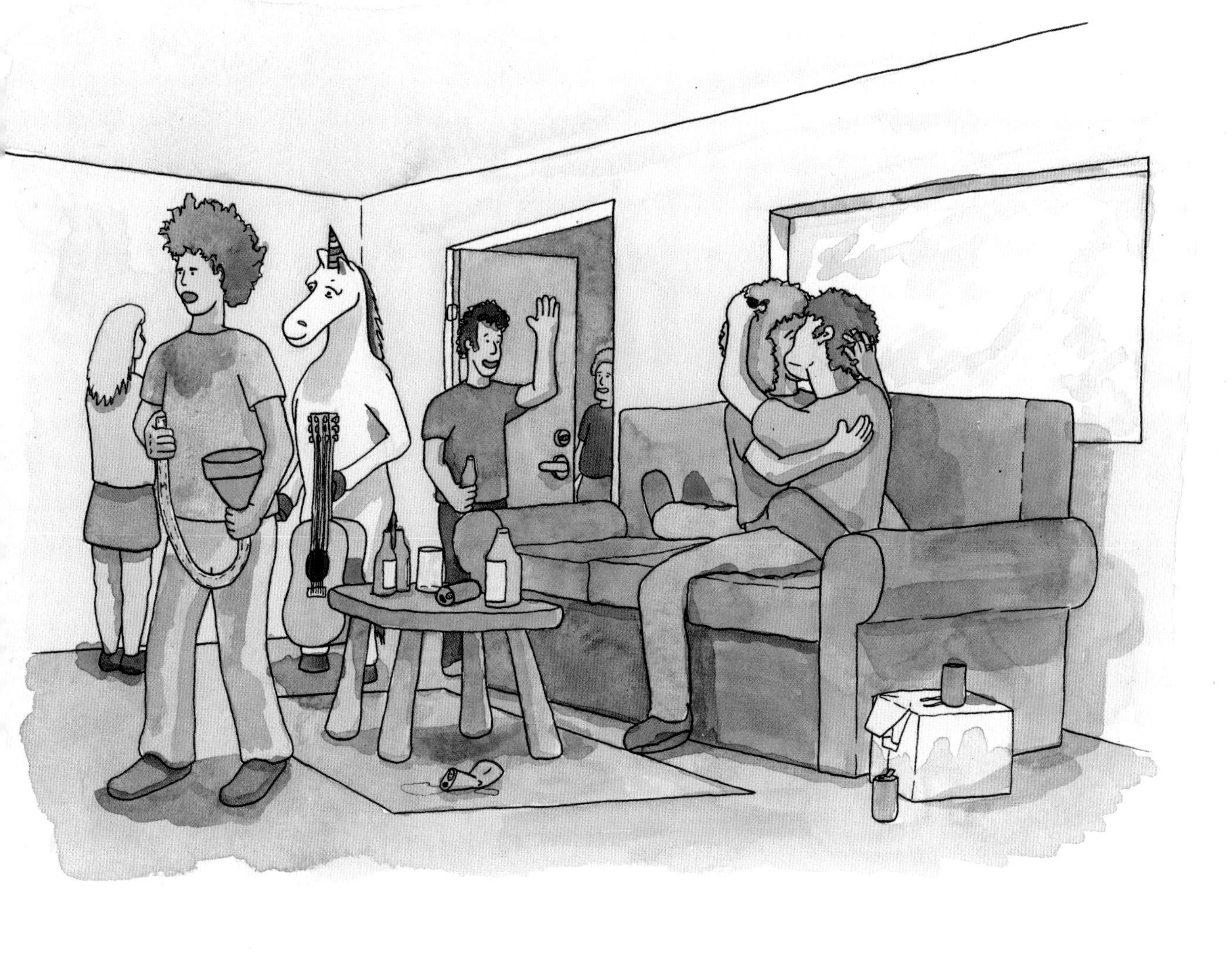

Burning ants with a magnifying glass.

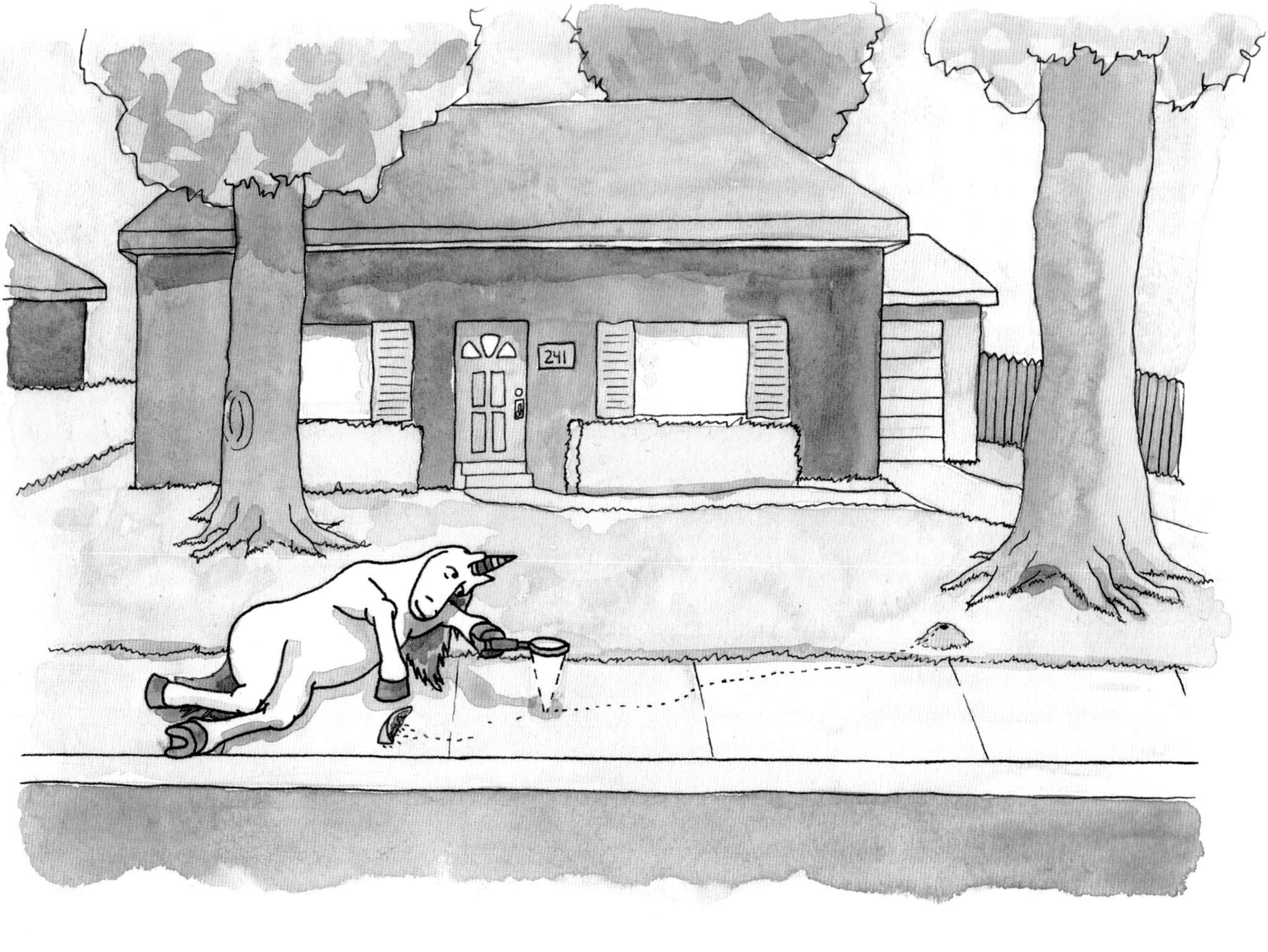
241

Cutting in line.

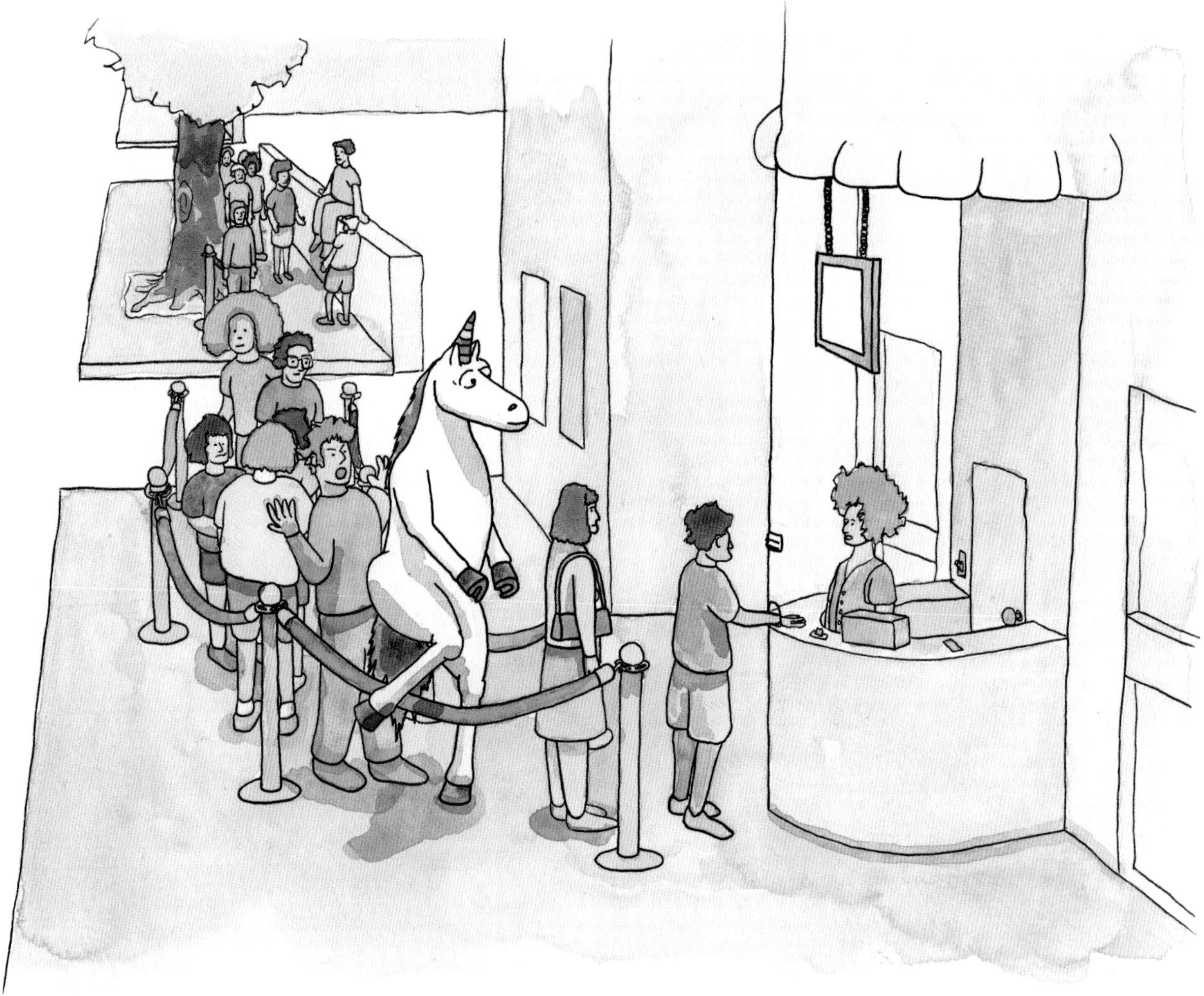

Tearing out the last page of a library book.

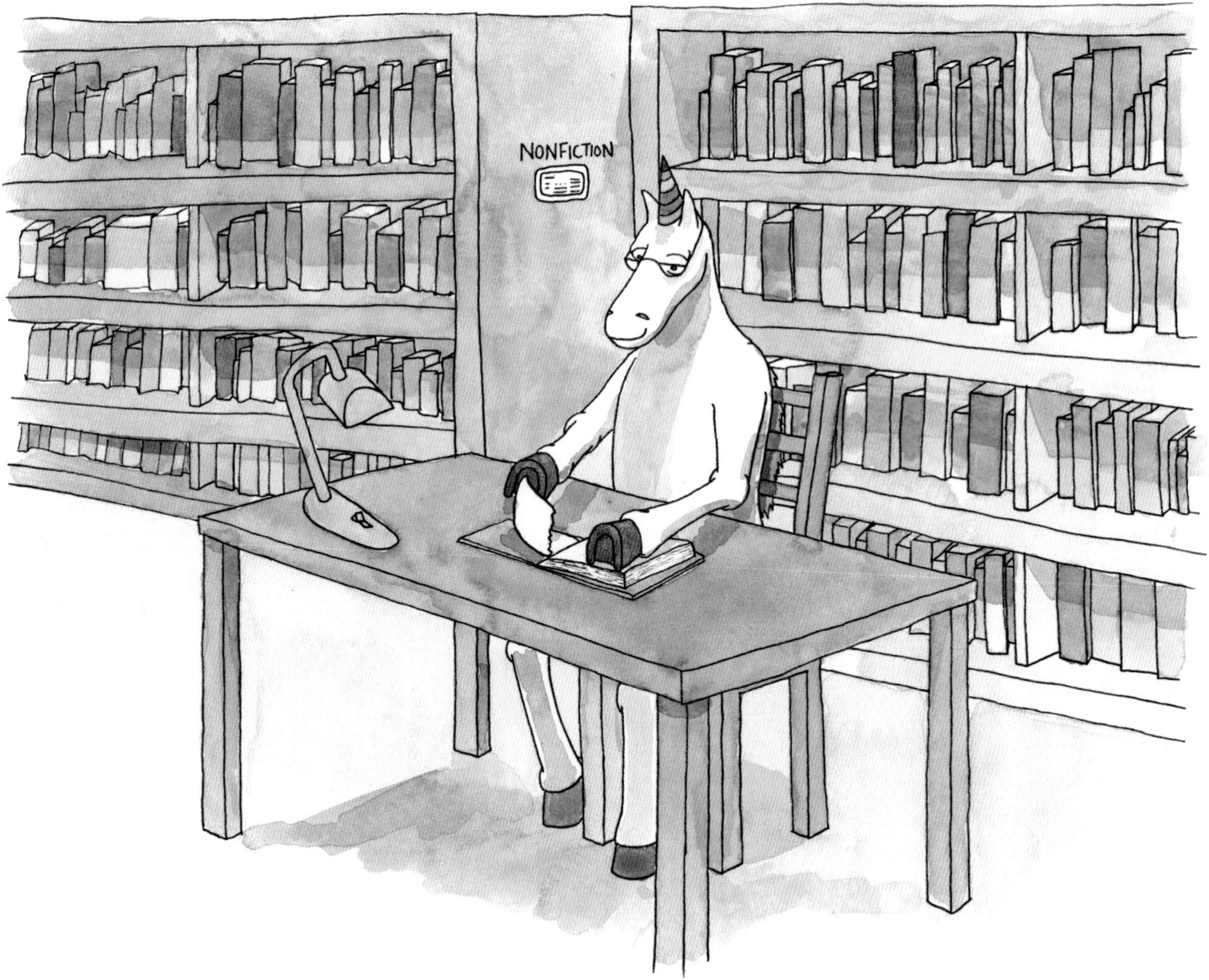
NONFICTION

Peeing in the pool.

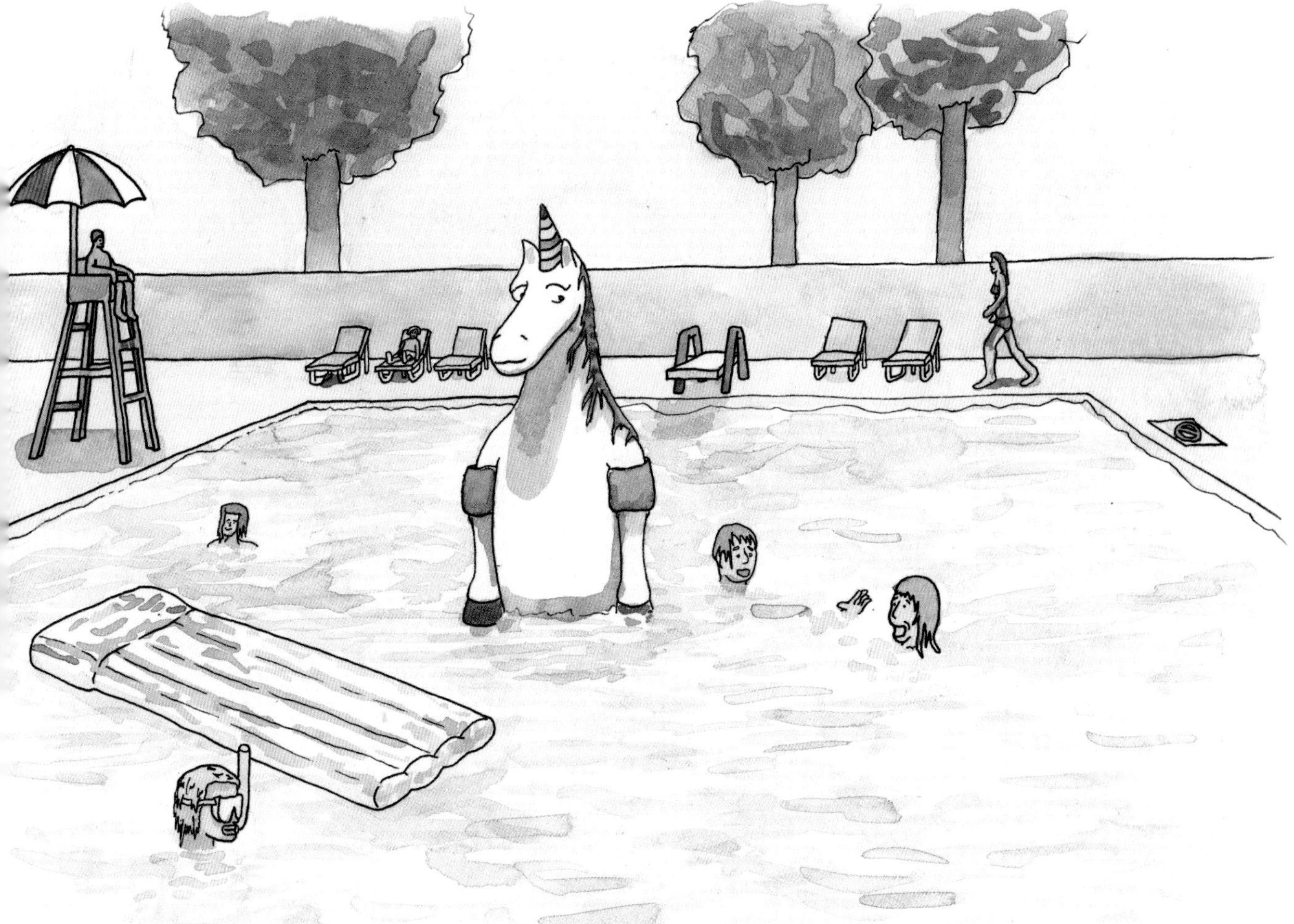

Putting a kitten in the microwave.

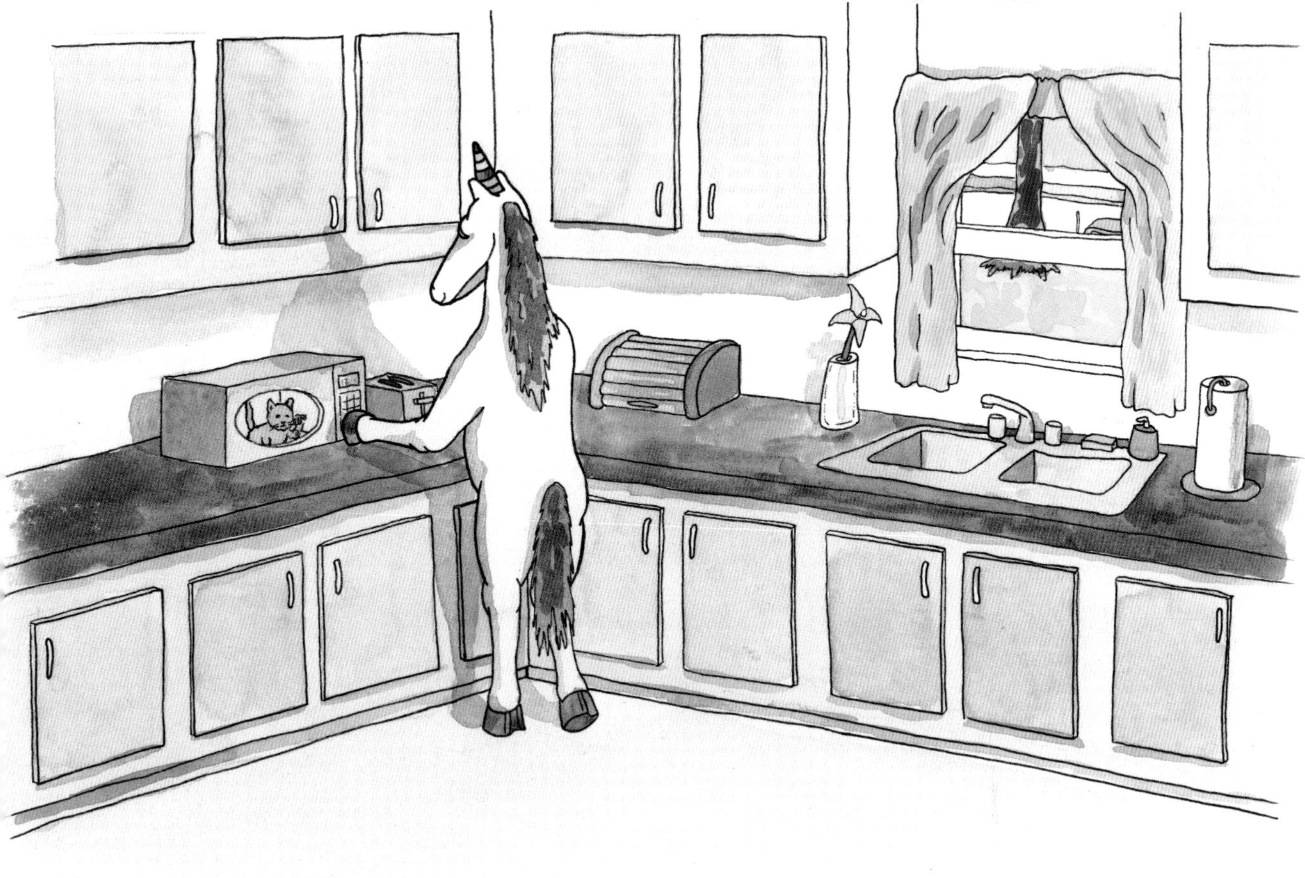

Raping America and its citizens for personal fiscal gain by creating fake market wealth in the stock exchange, real estate market, and currency trade—then expecting the people of America to bail him out.

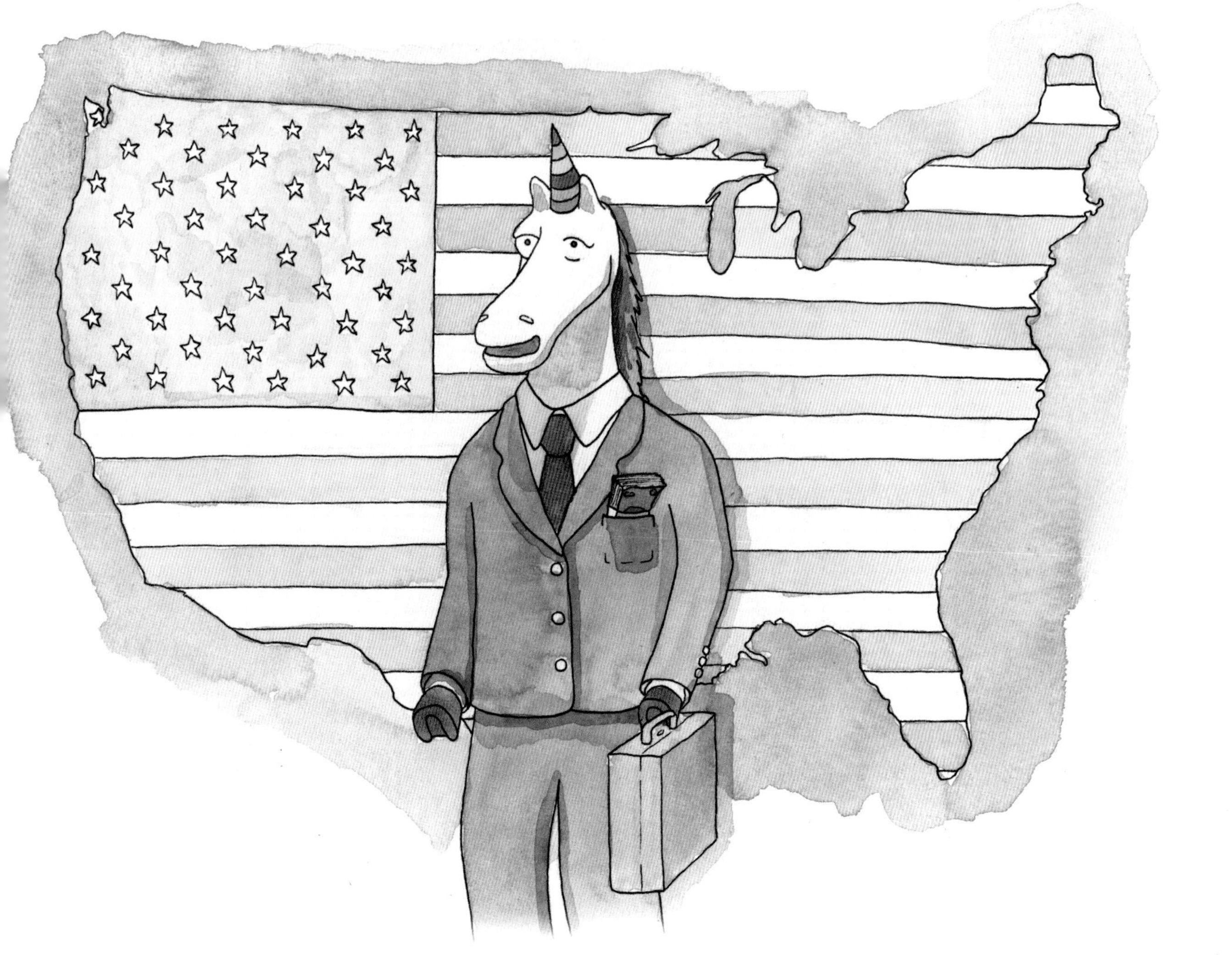

Teepeeing someone's home.

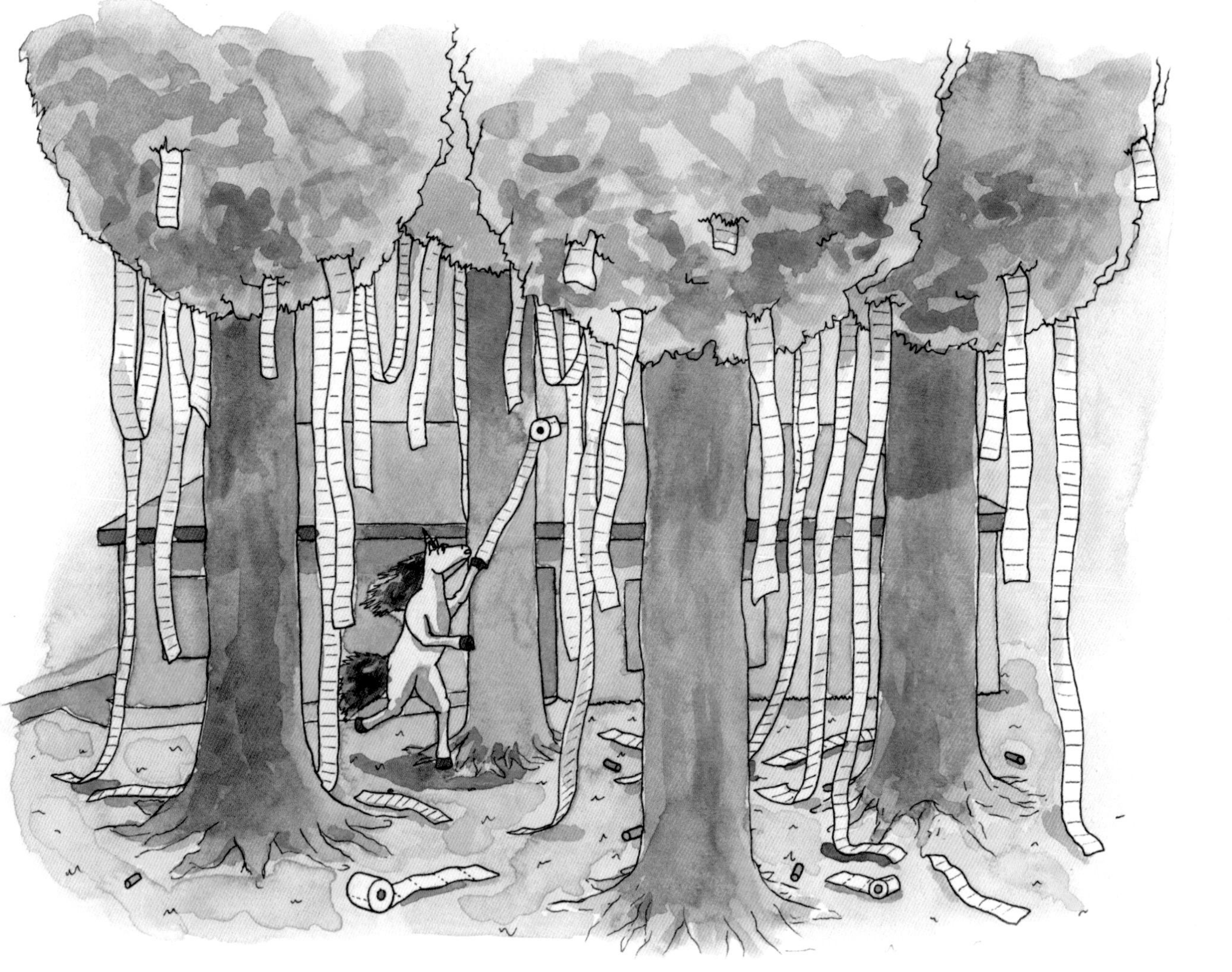

Judging his daughter's boyfriend.

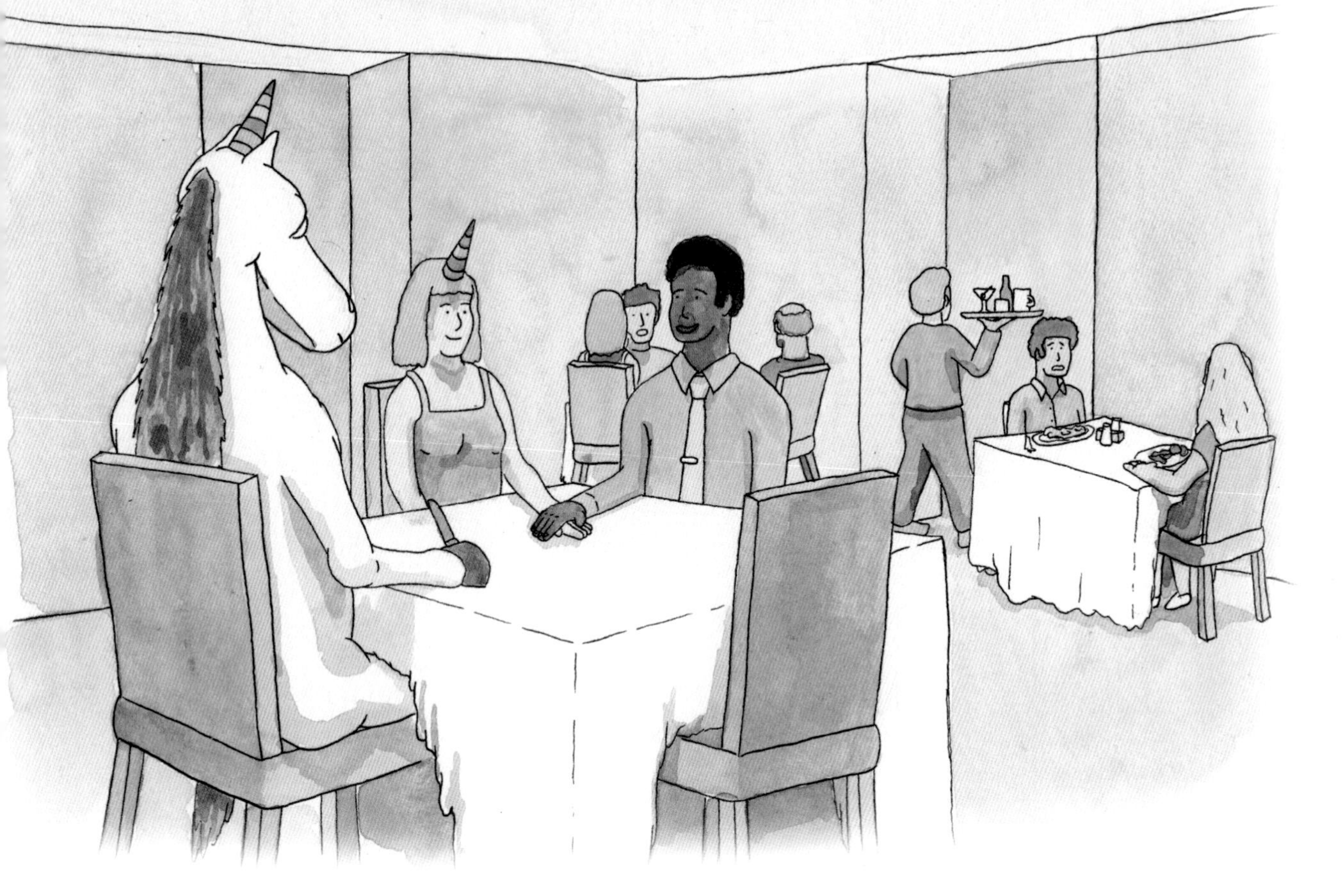

Pushing the close button.

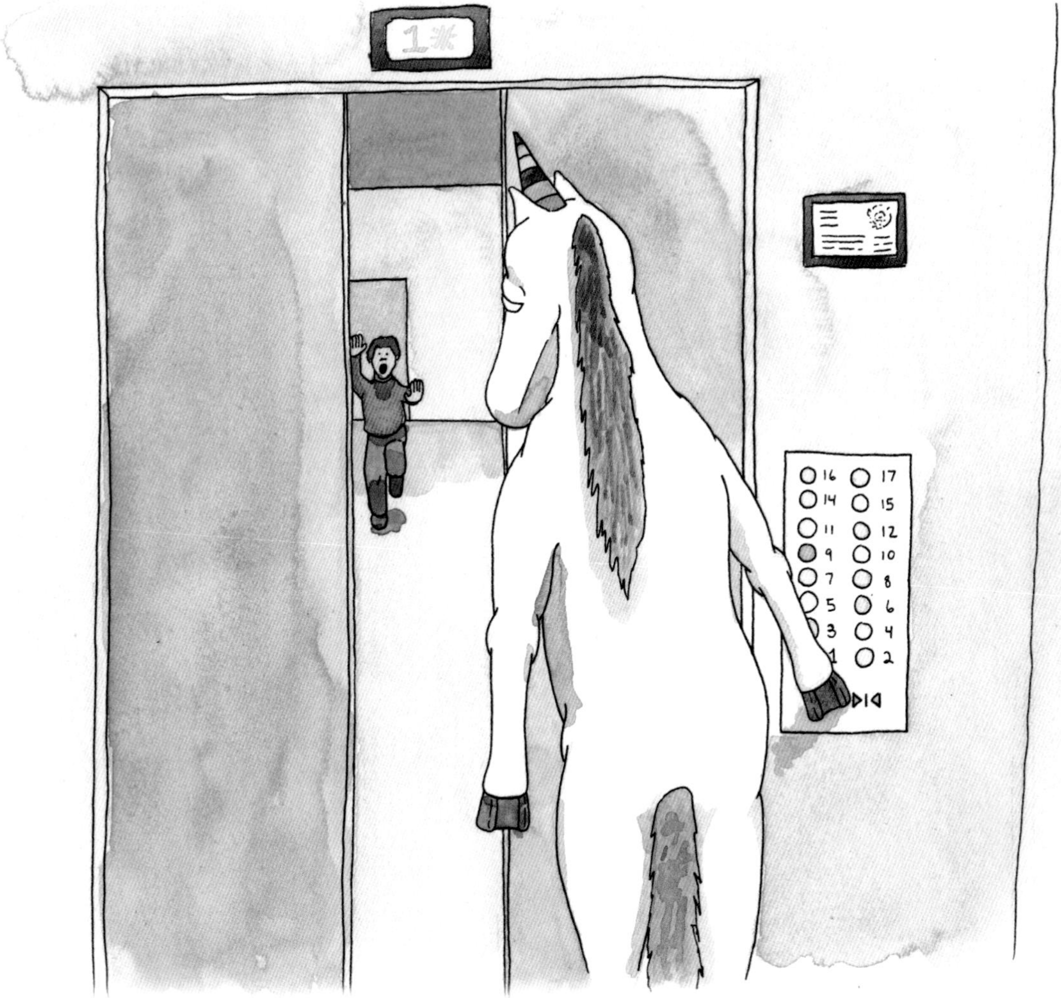
16 17
14 15
11 12
9 10
7 8
5 6
3 4
1 2

Clubbing baby seals.

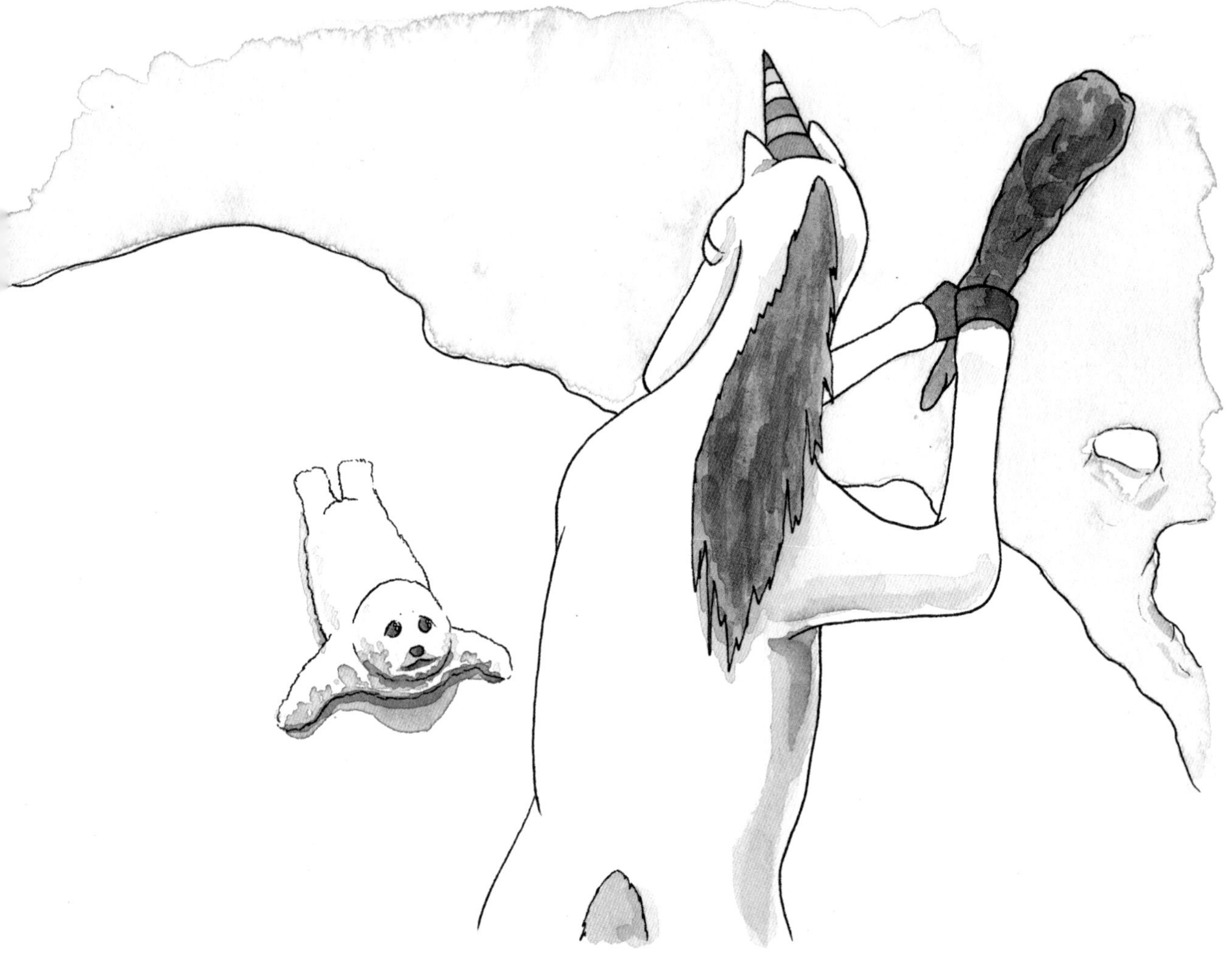

Walking his child on a leash.

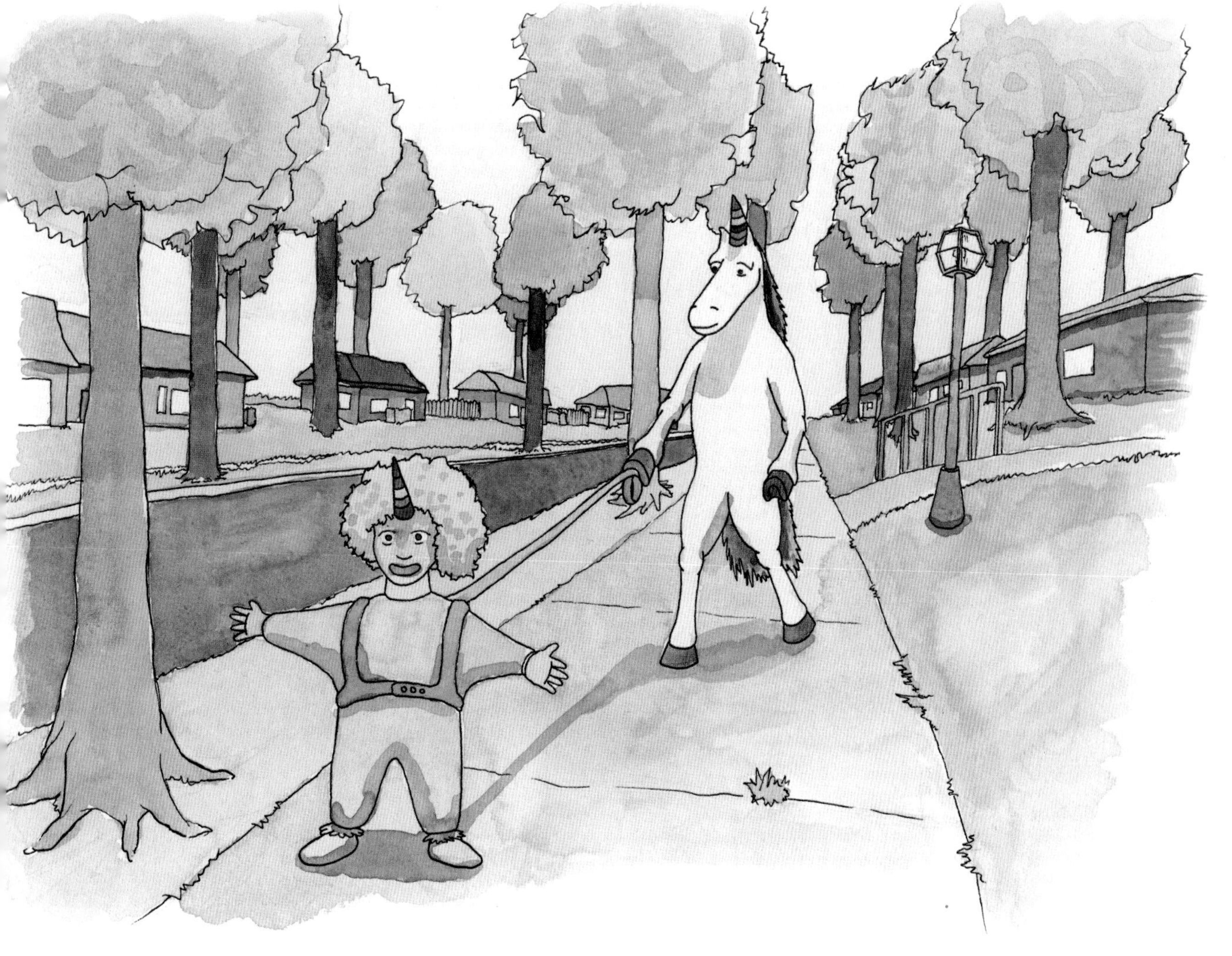

Fiddling with his cell phone while on a date.

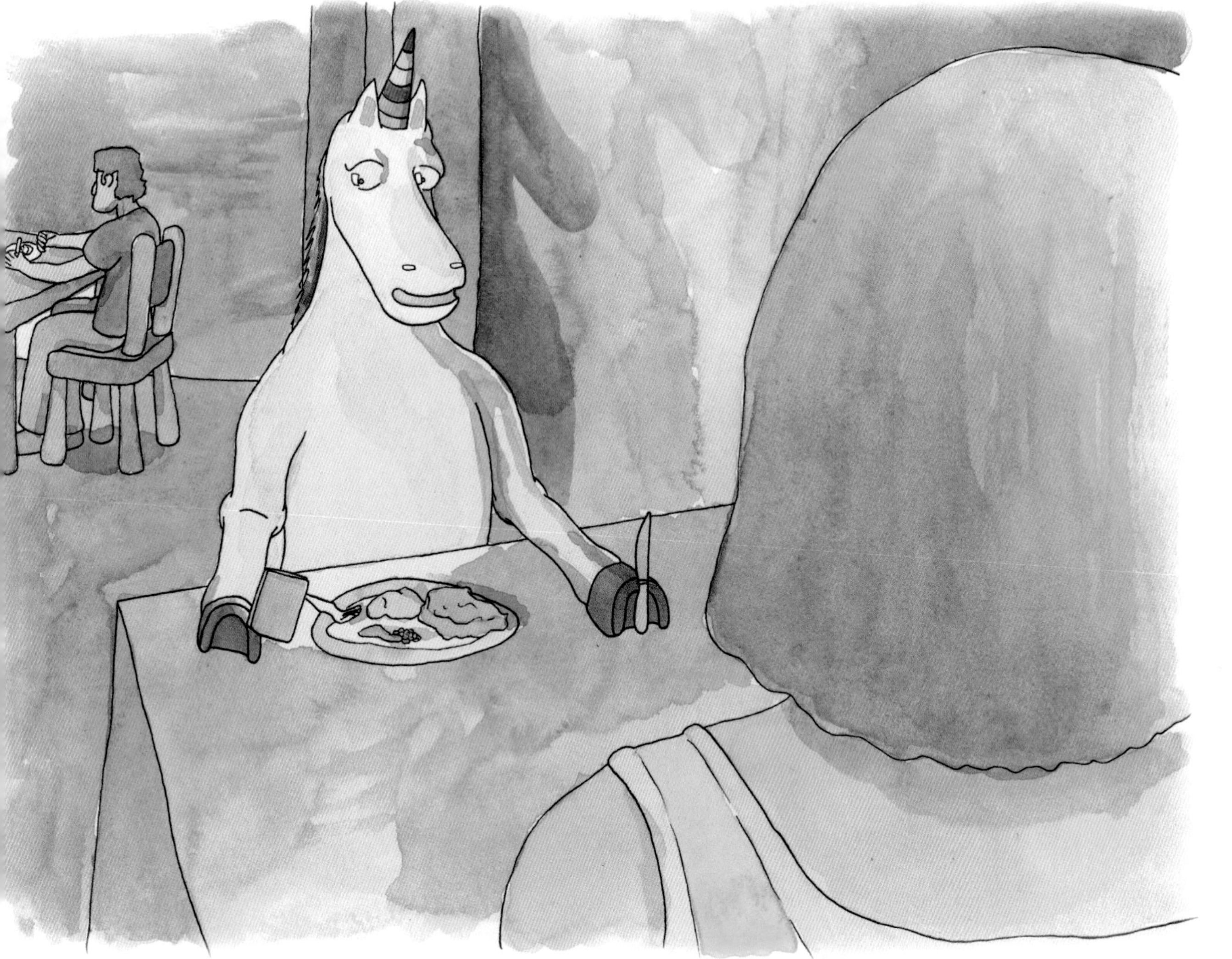

Hoping his son isn't gay.

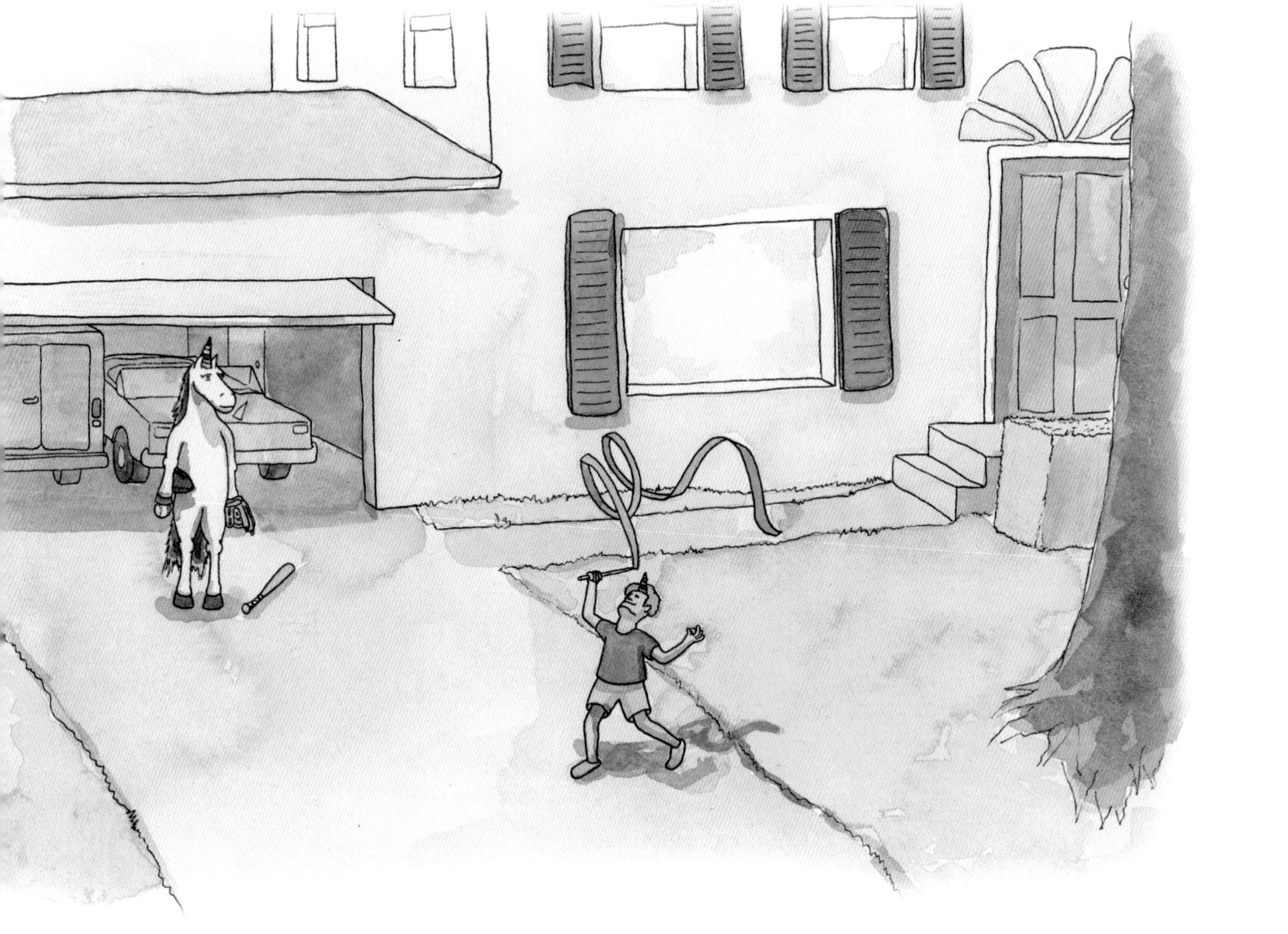

Teasing animals at the zoo.

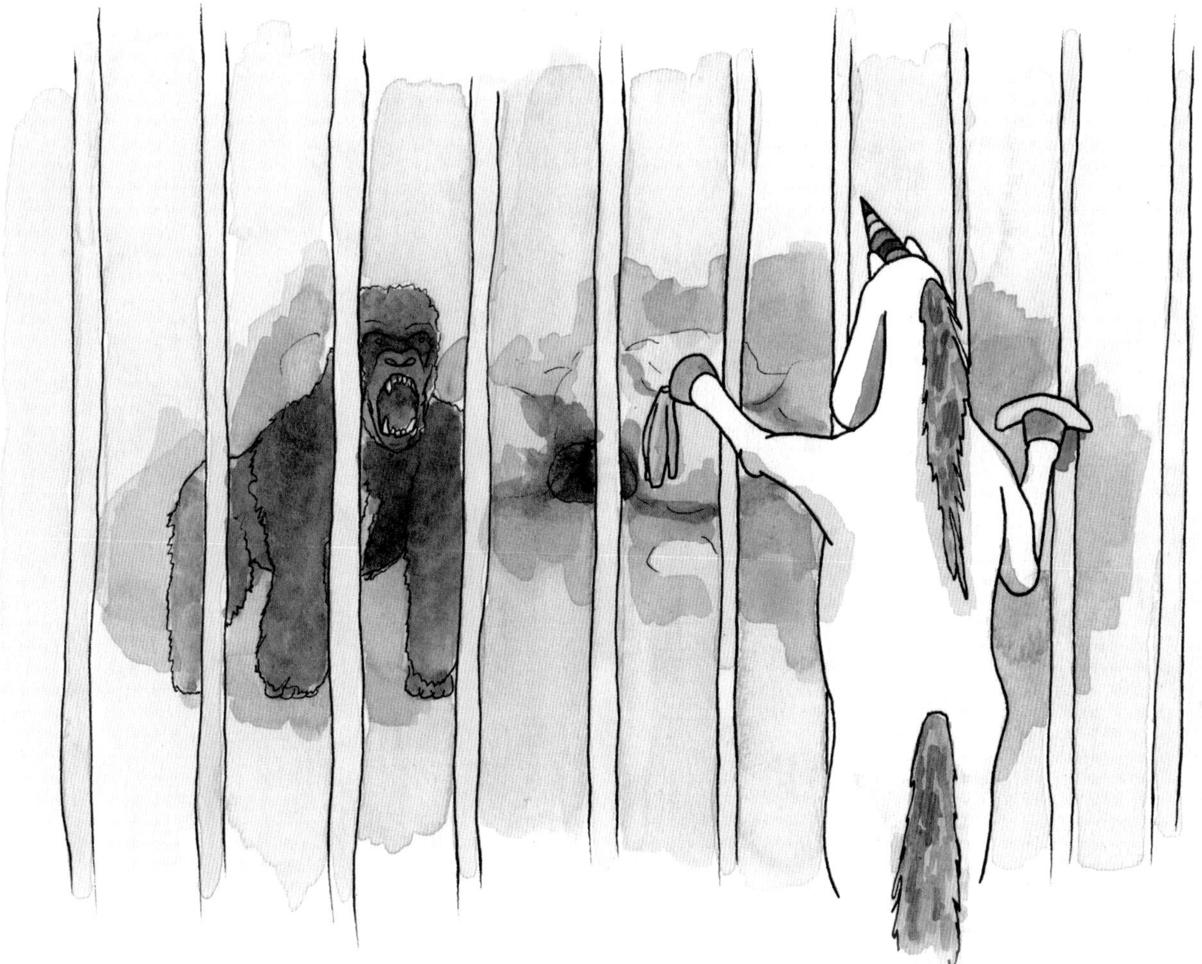

Parking in the last empty handicap spot.

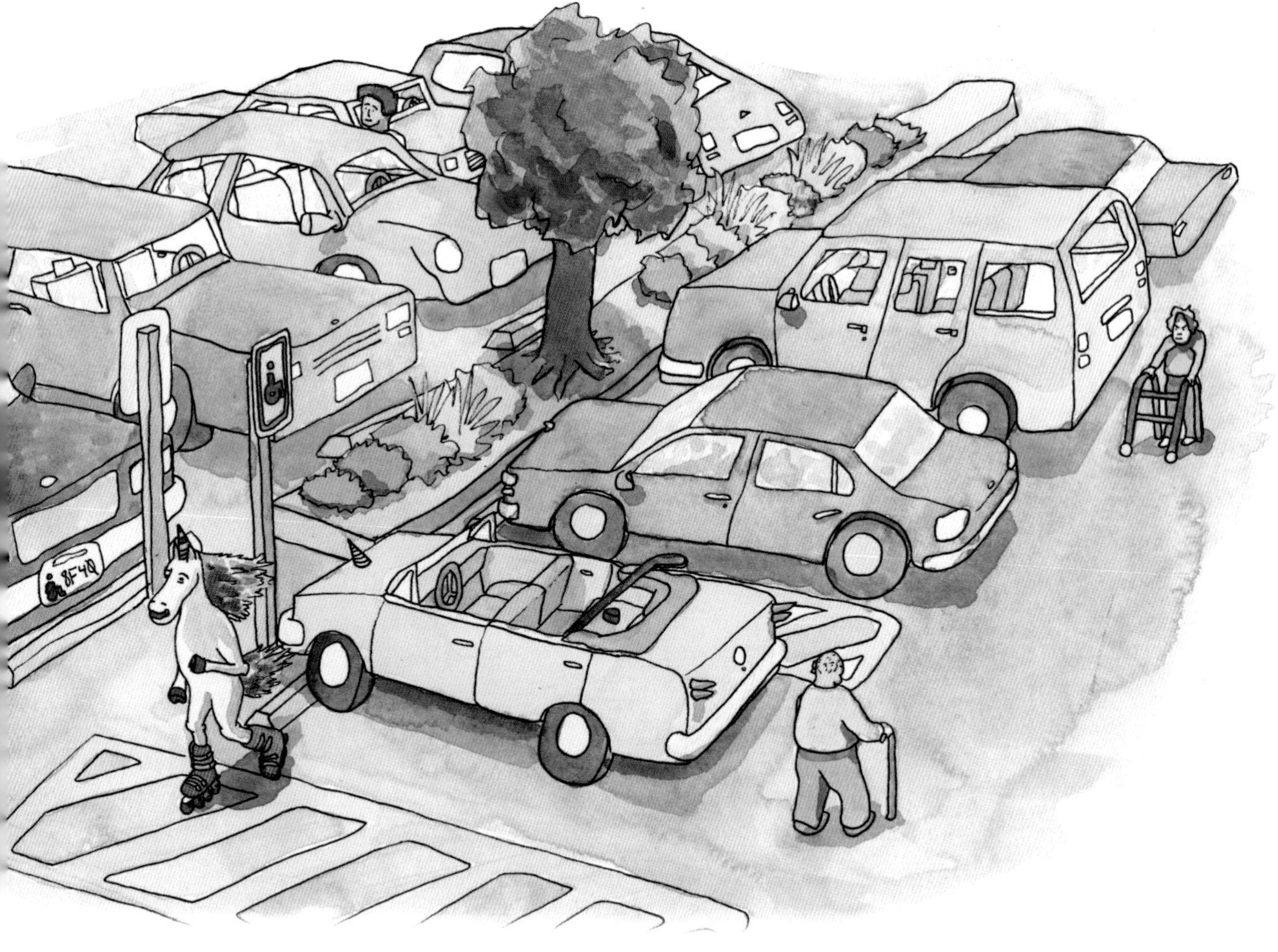
8F4Q

Being a bully.

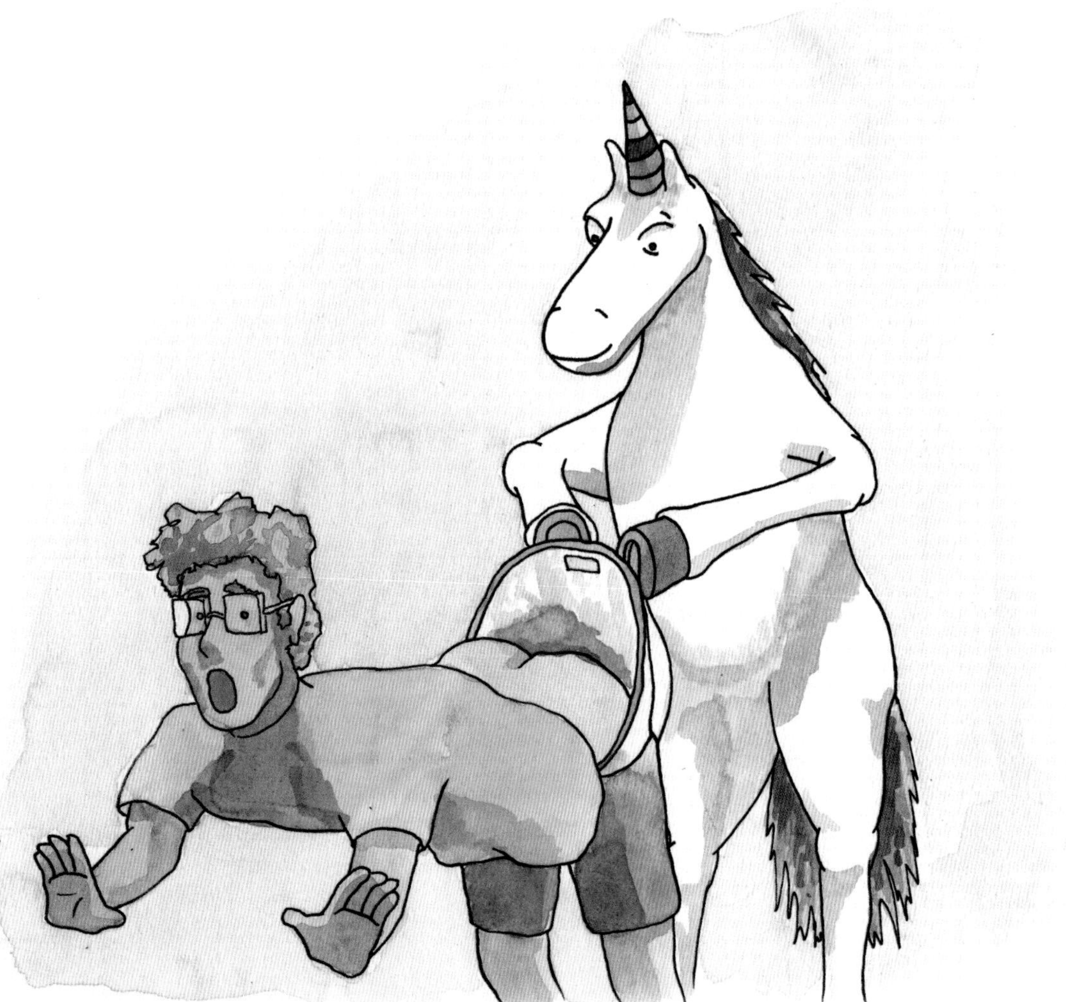

Photocopying his rear end.

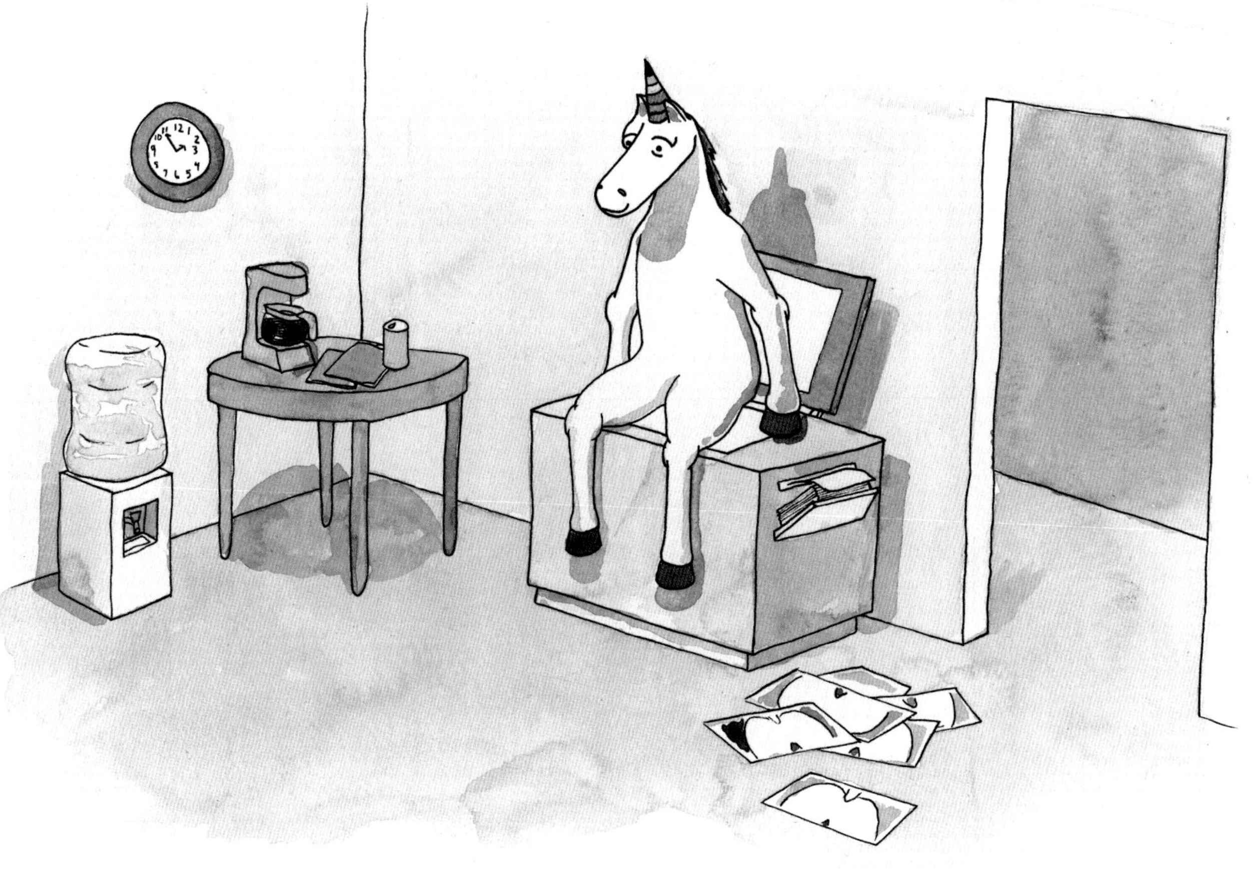

Abusing his wife.

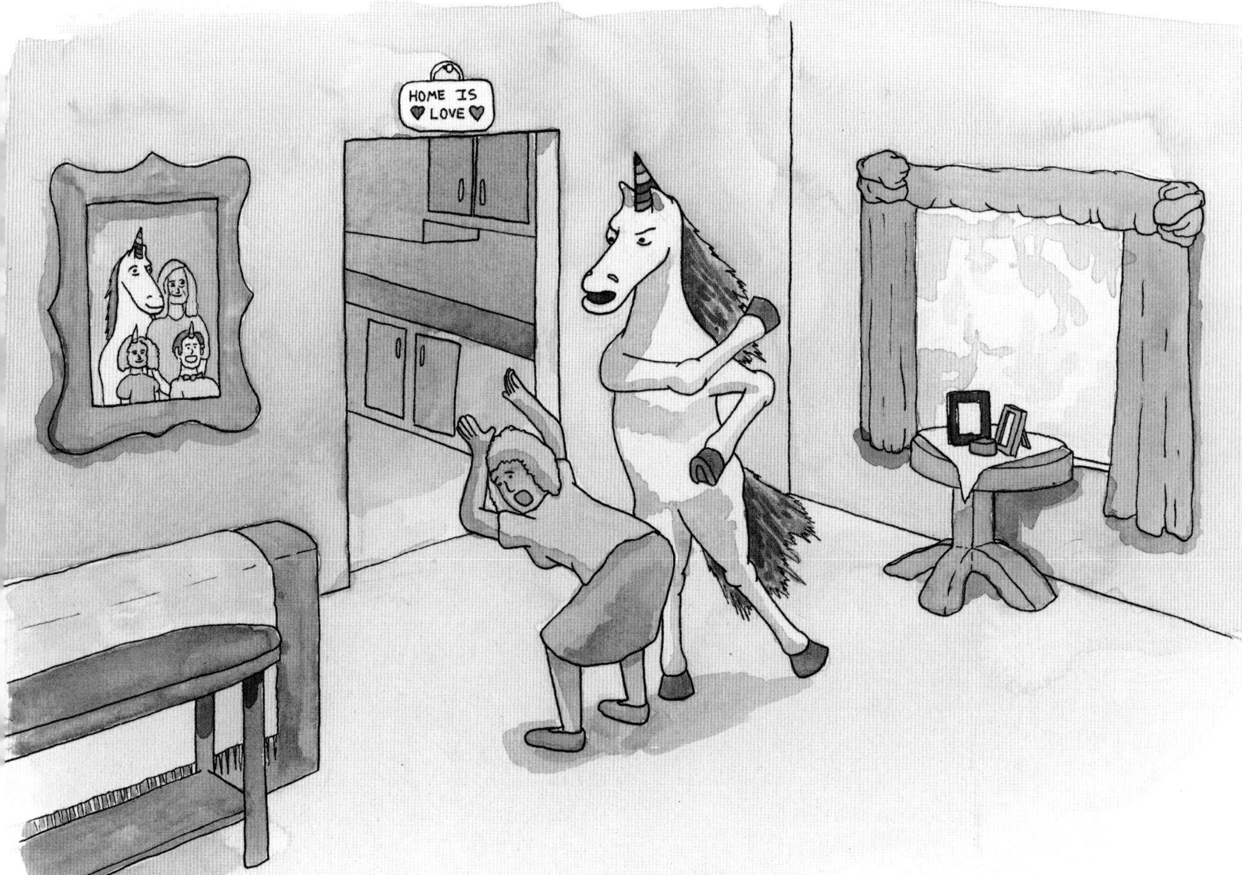
HOME IS
LOVE

Tagging the side of the building.

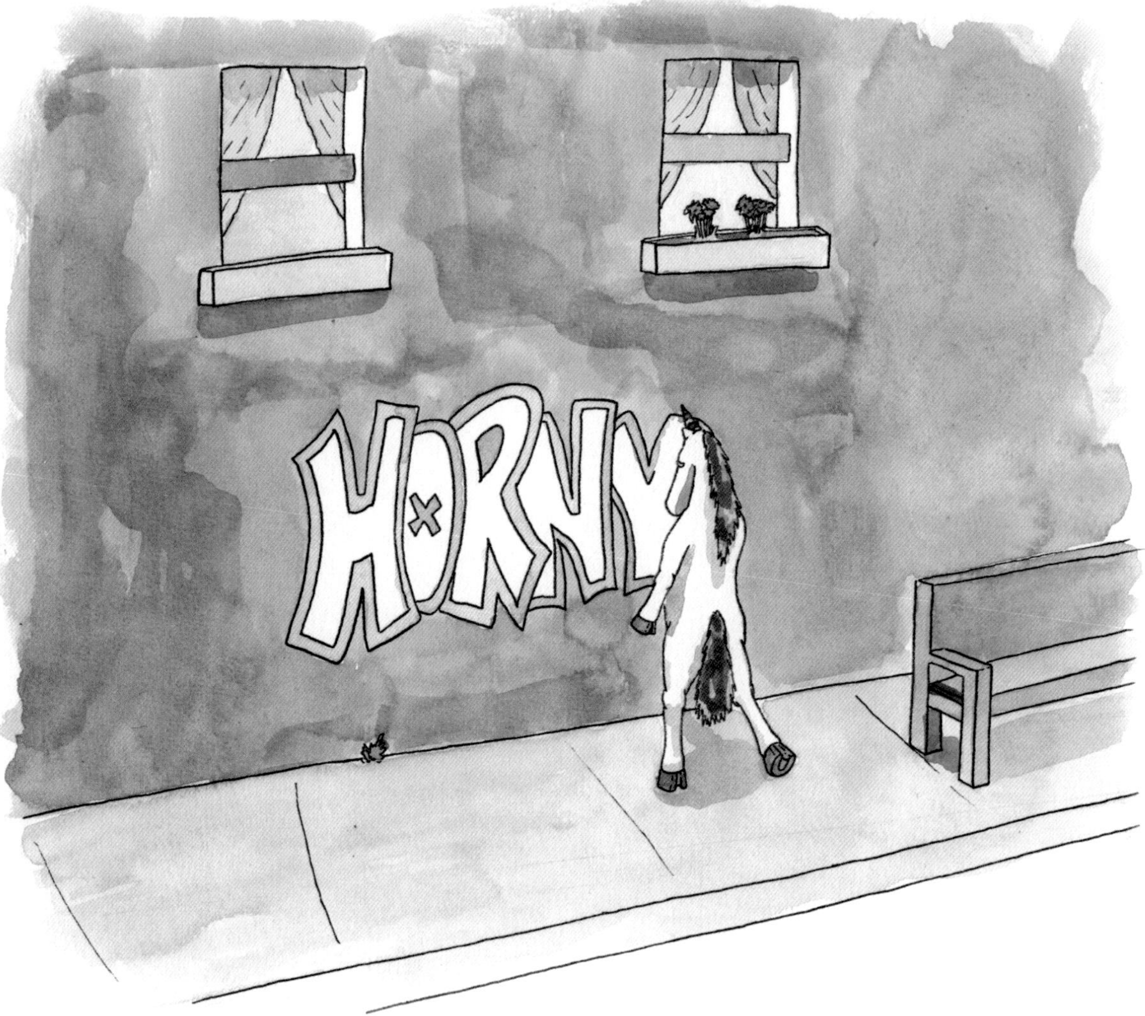
HORNY

Writing a Wikipedia® page about himself.

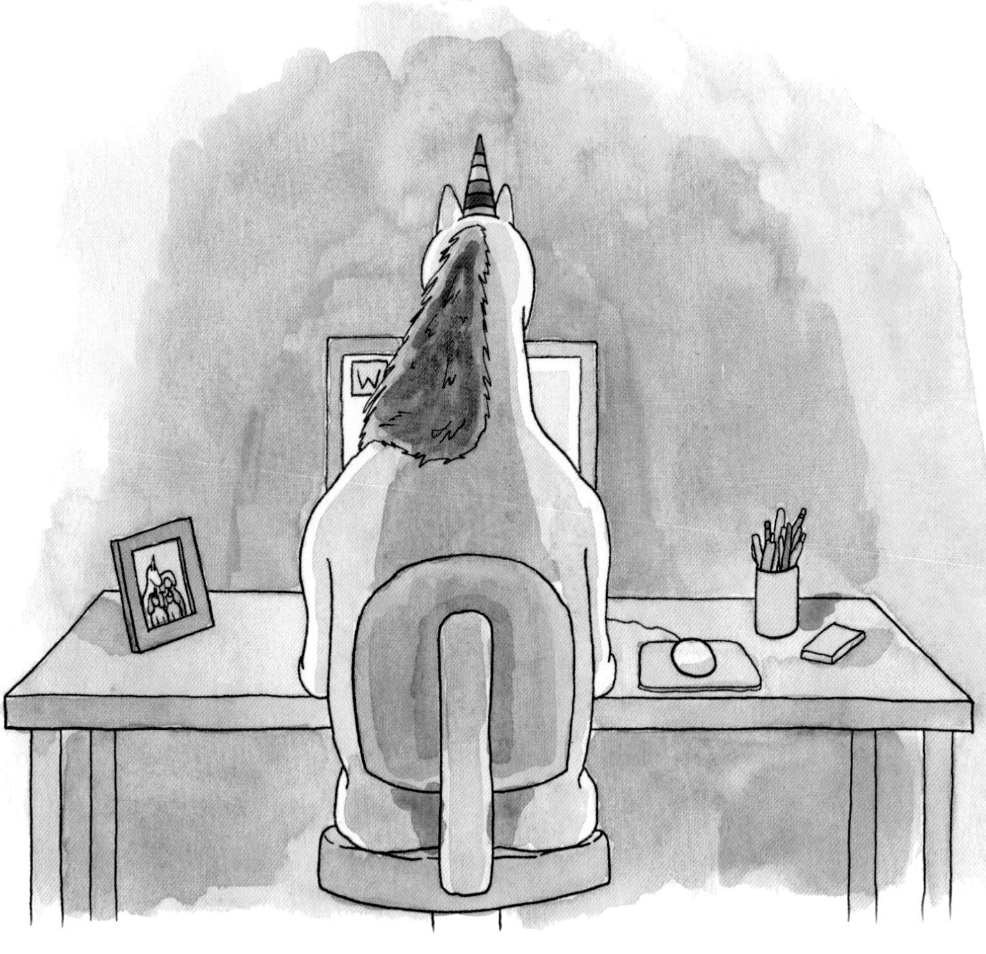

Talking about fashion in a sports bar.

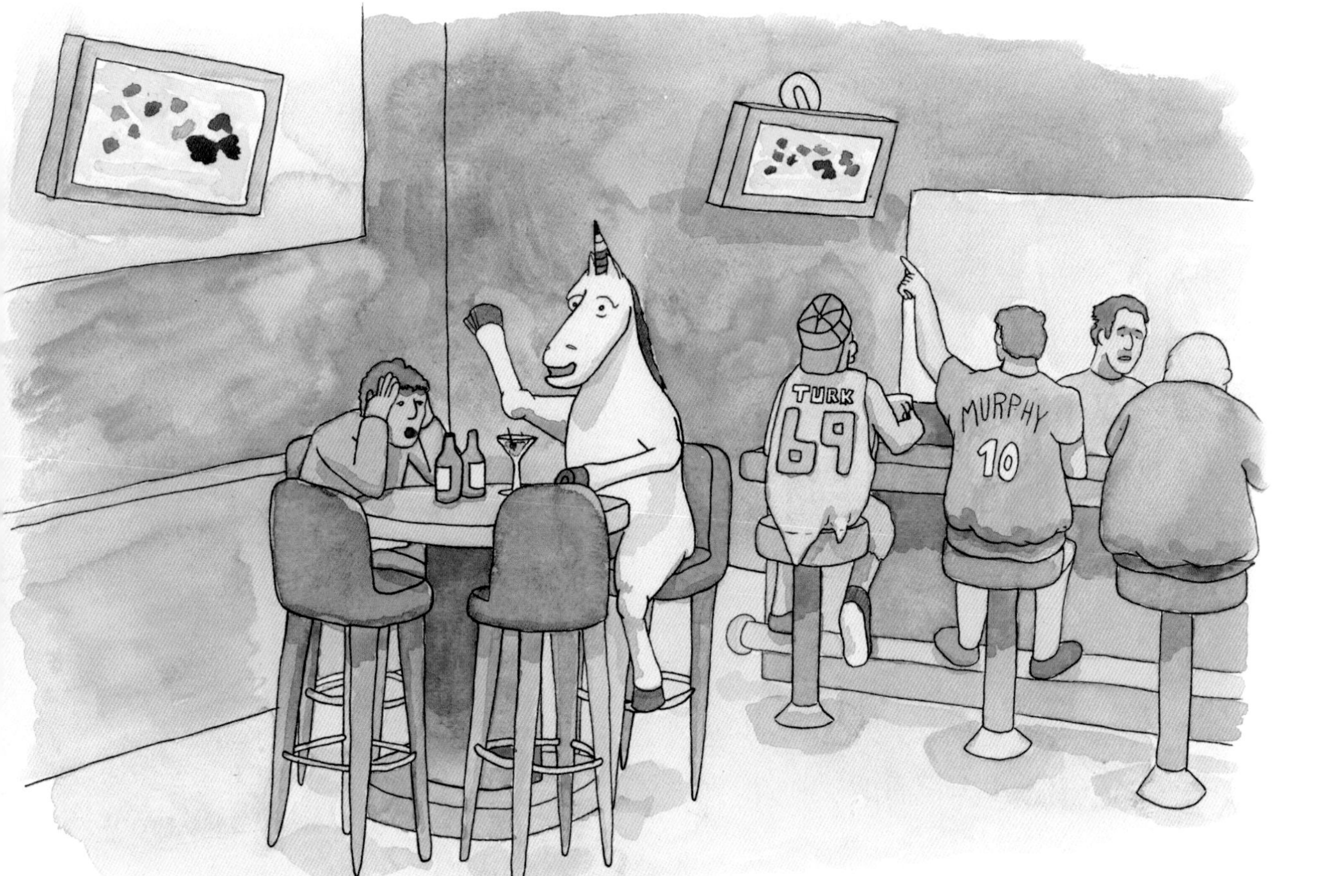
TURK
69
MURPHY
10

Pushing his religion on others.

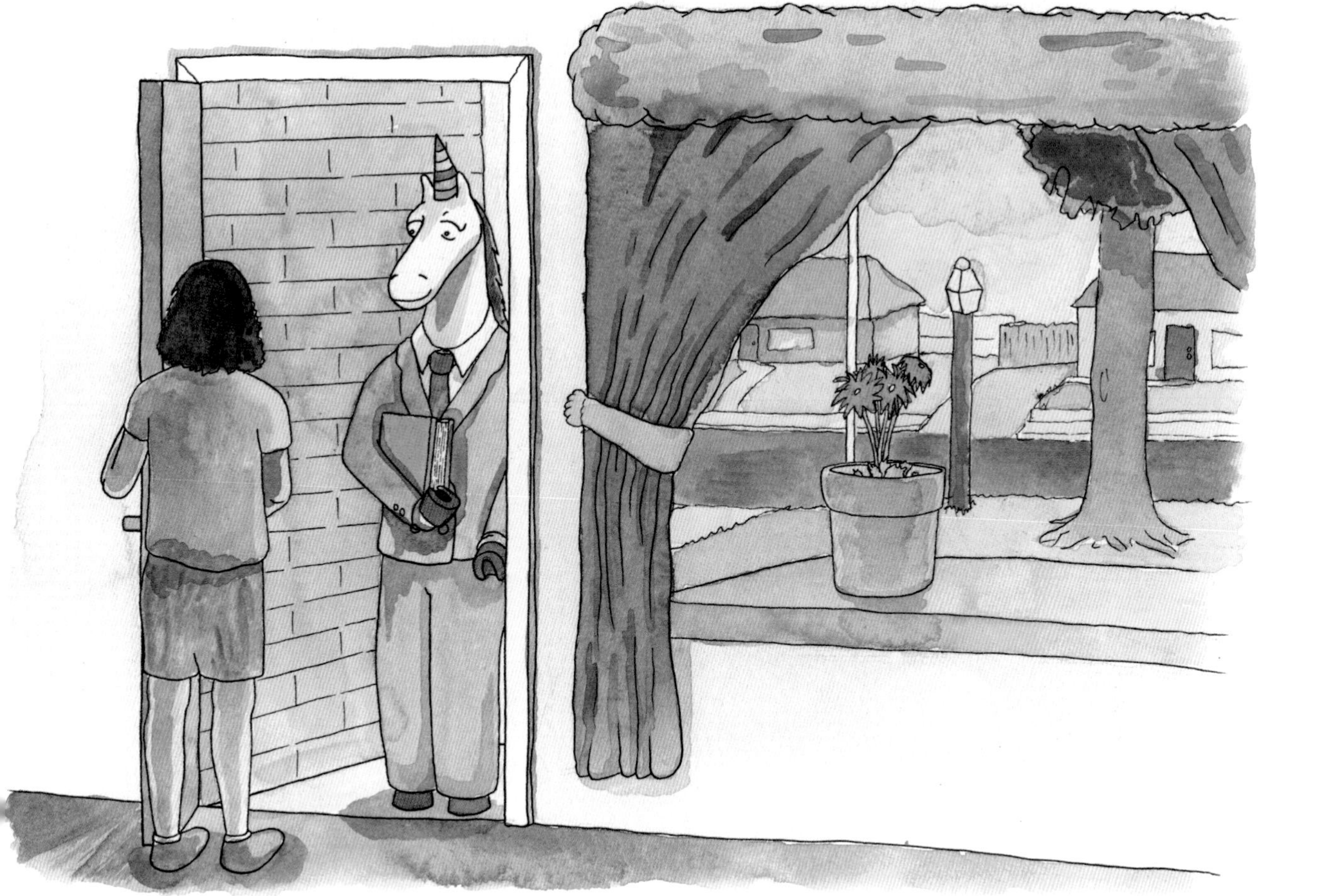

Writing in wet cement.

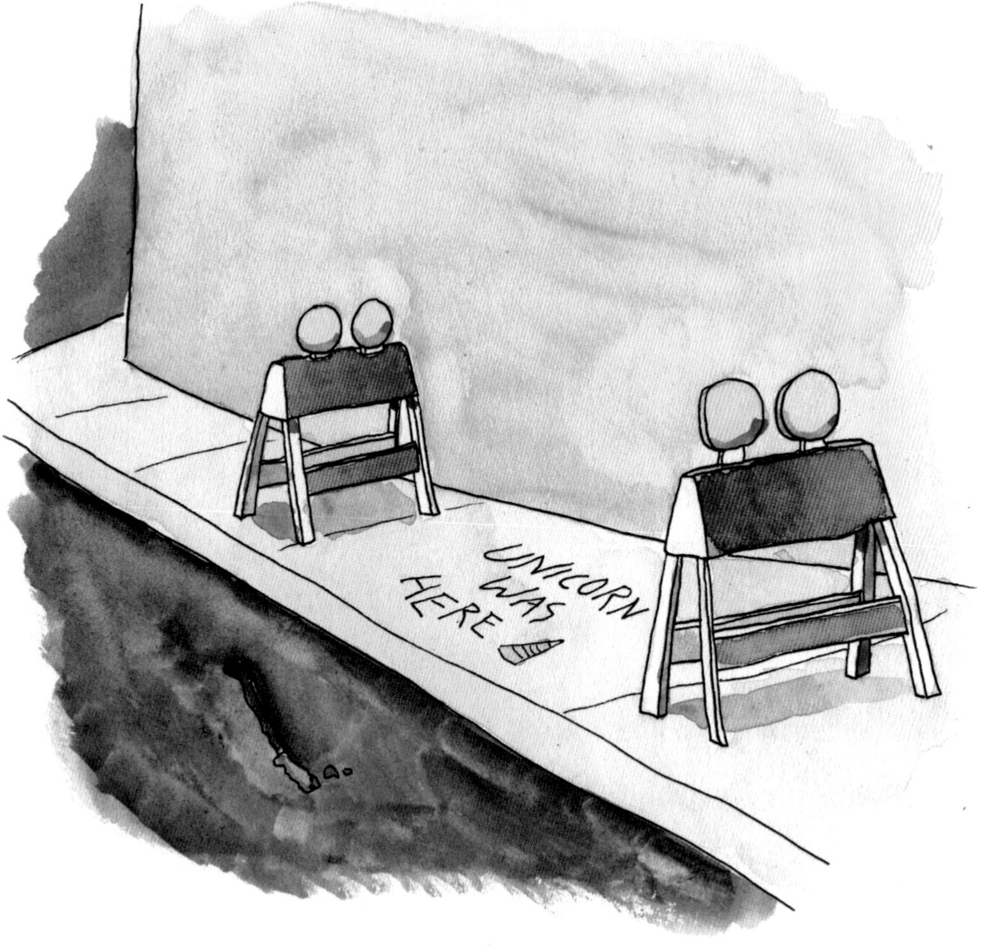
UNICORN
WAS
HERE

Being a stalker.

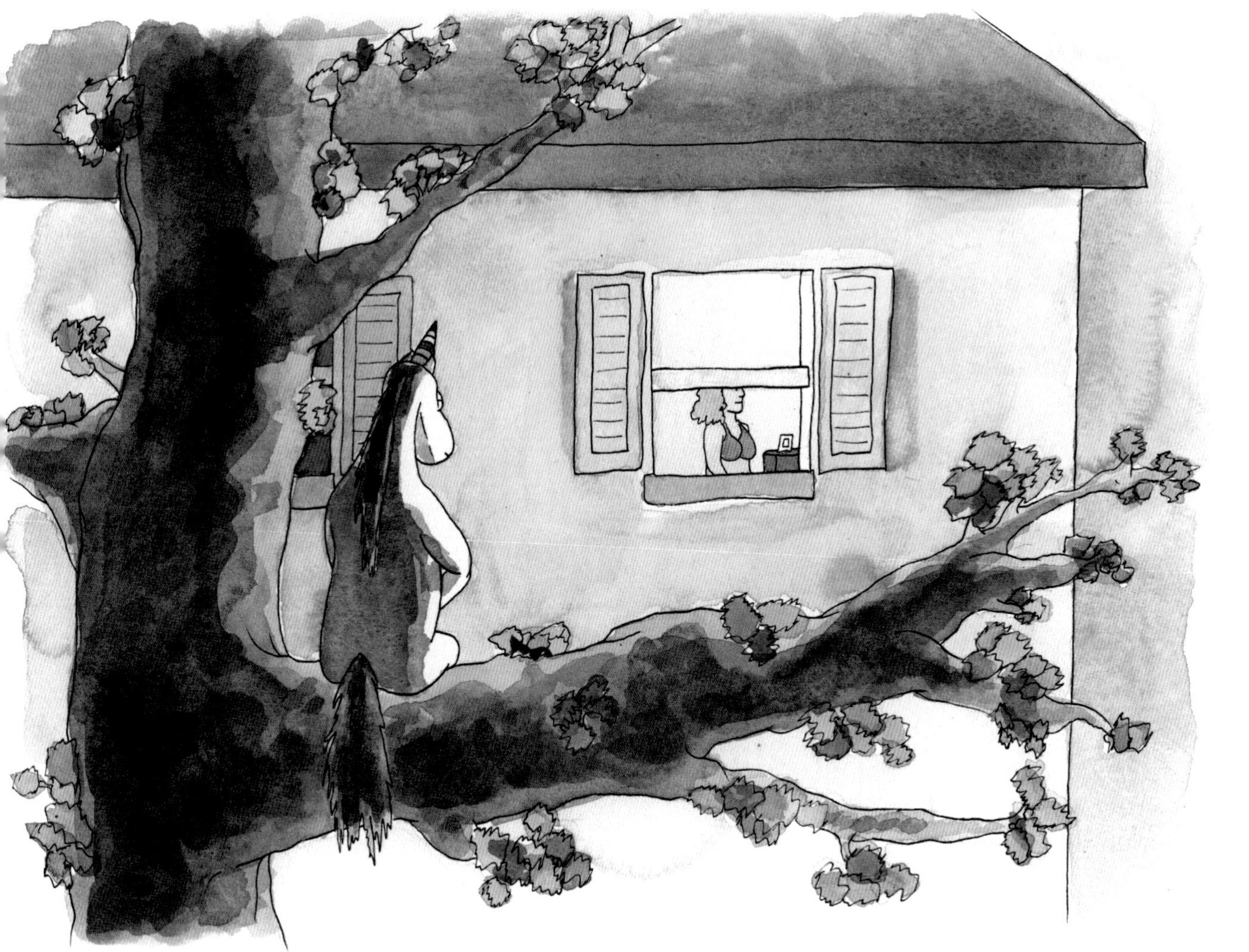

Feeding pigs bacon.

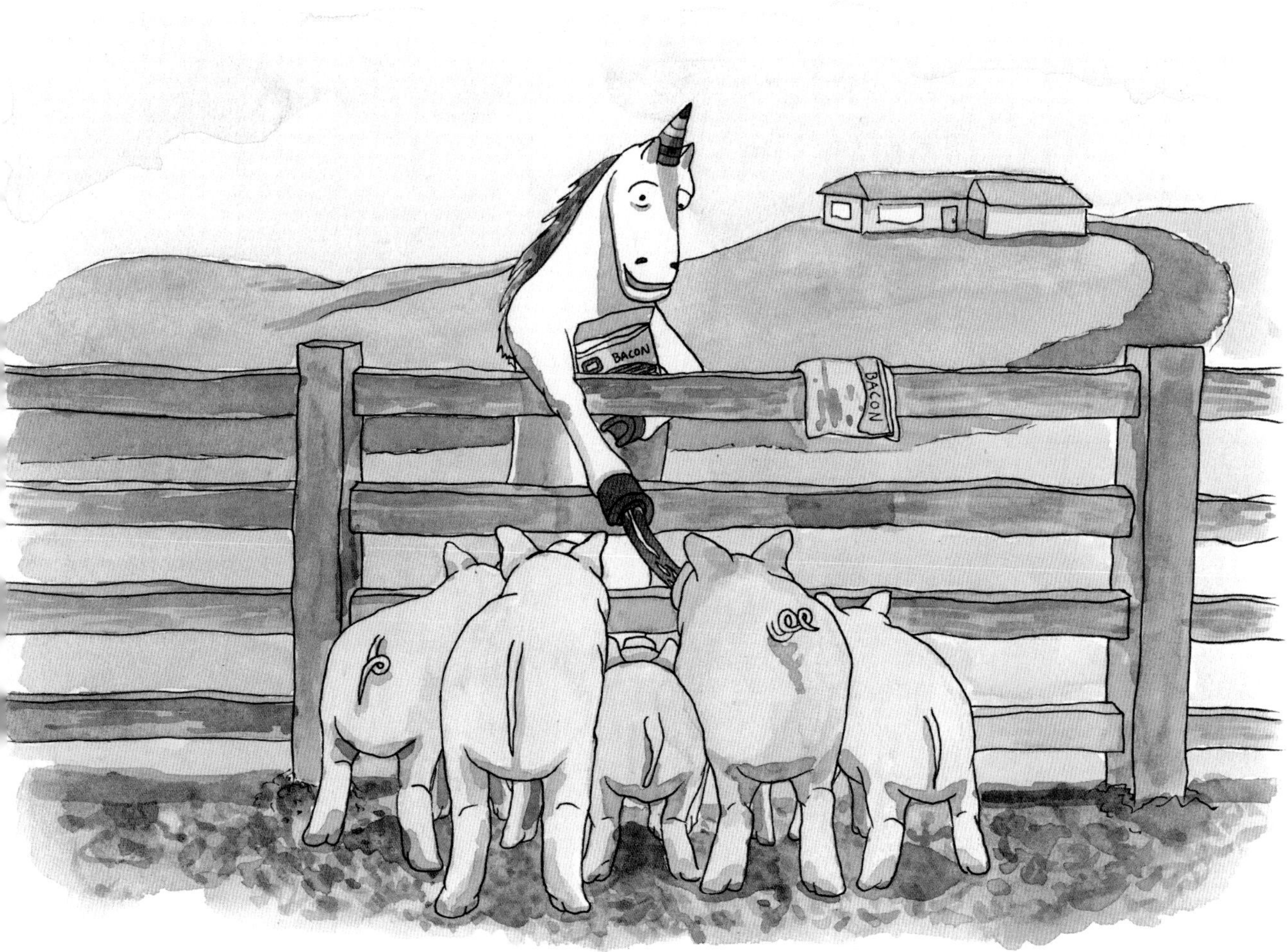
BACON
BACON

Being a pedophile.

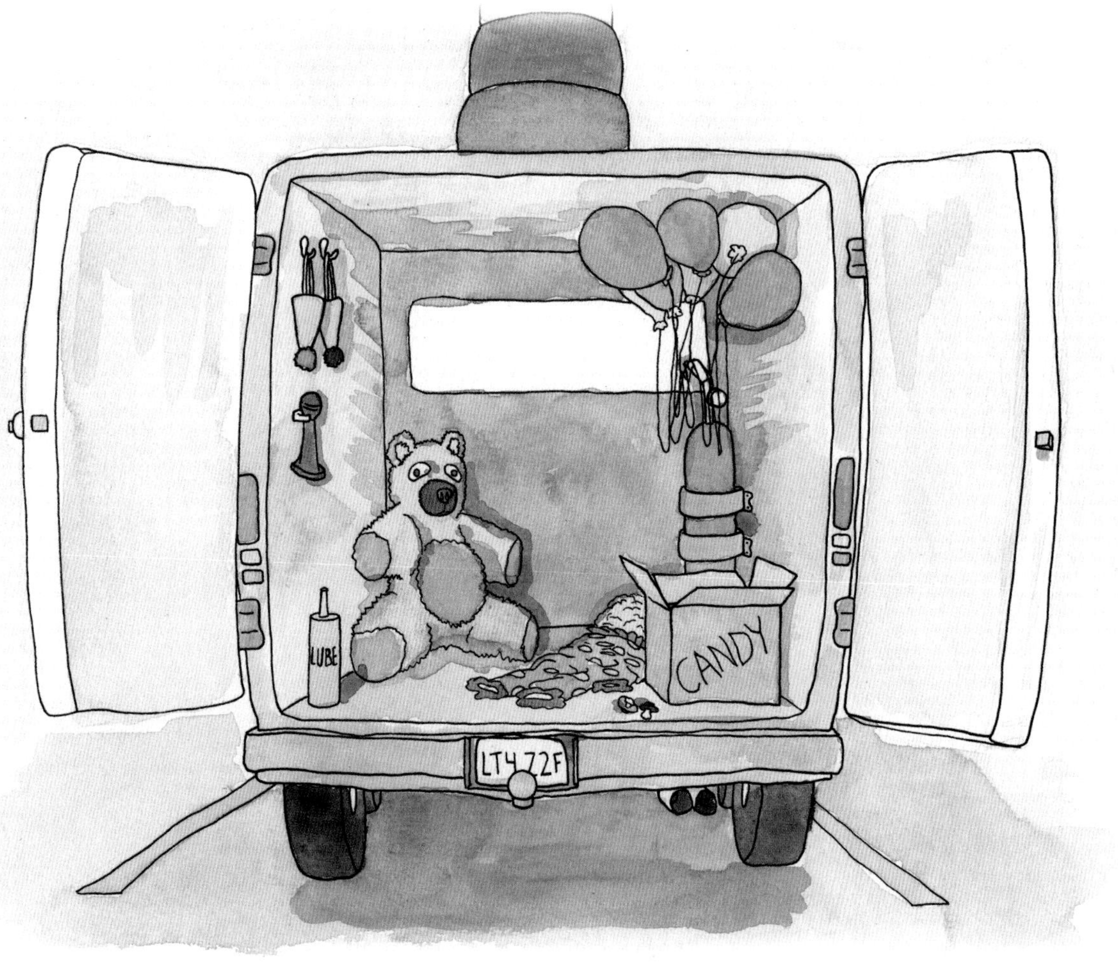
LUBE
CANDY
LT4 72F

Reading his daughter's diary.

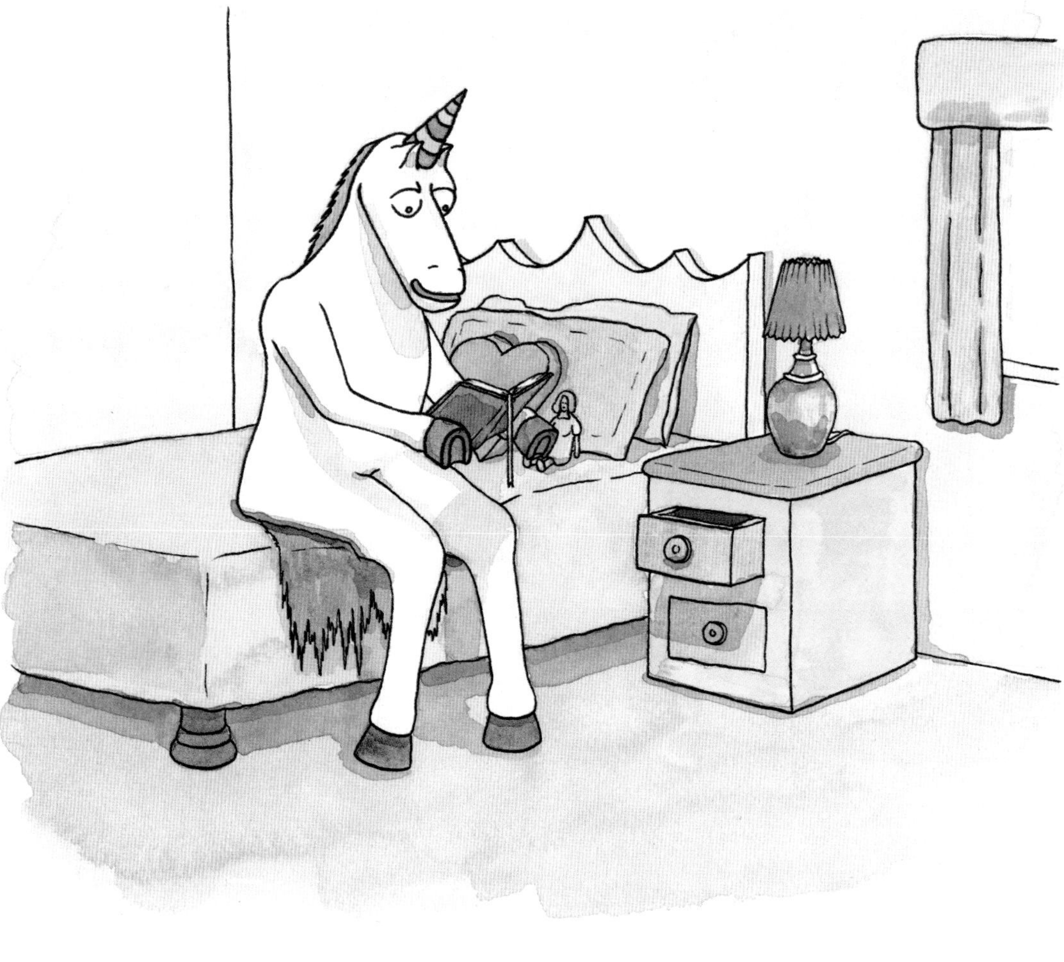

Hanging photos only of himself.

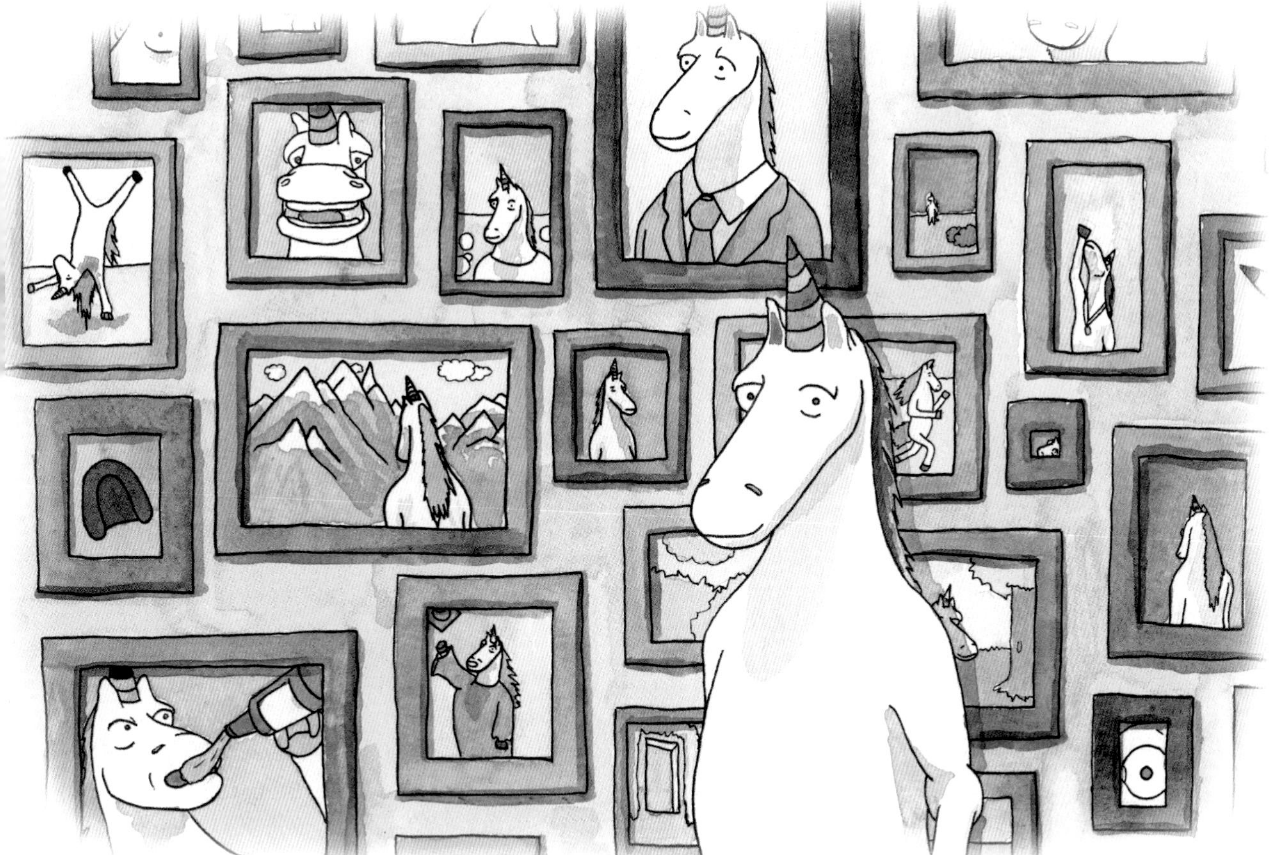

Making potholes.

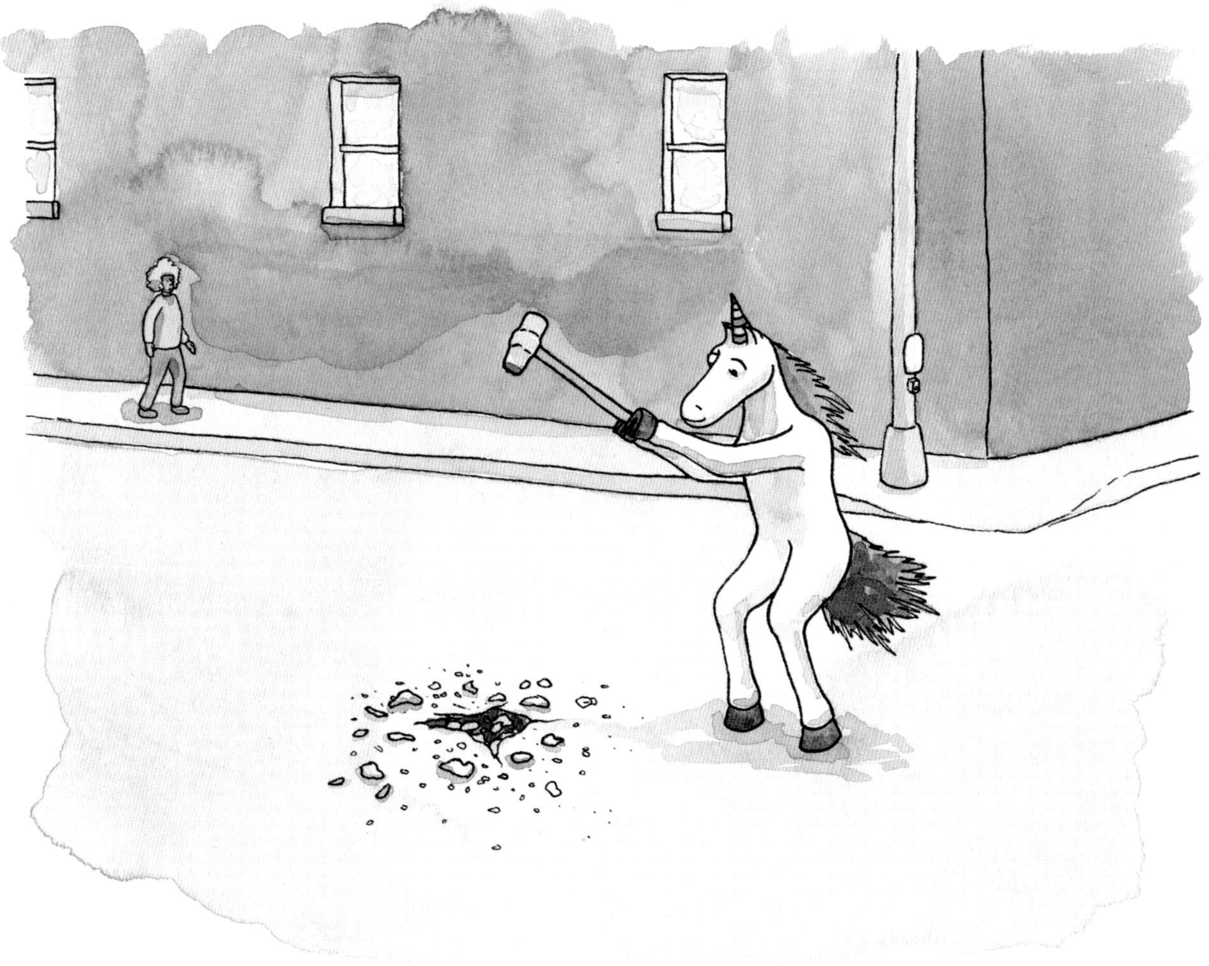

Making fake treasure maps that
lead to his torture chamber.

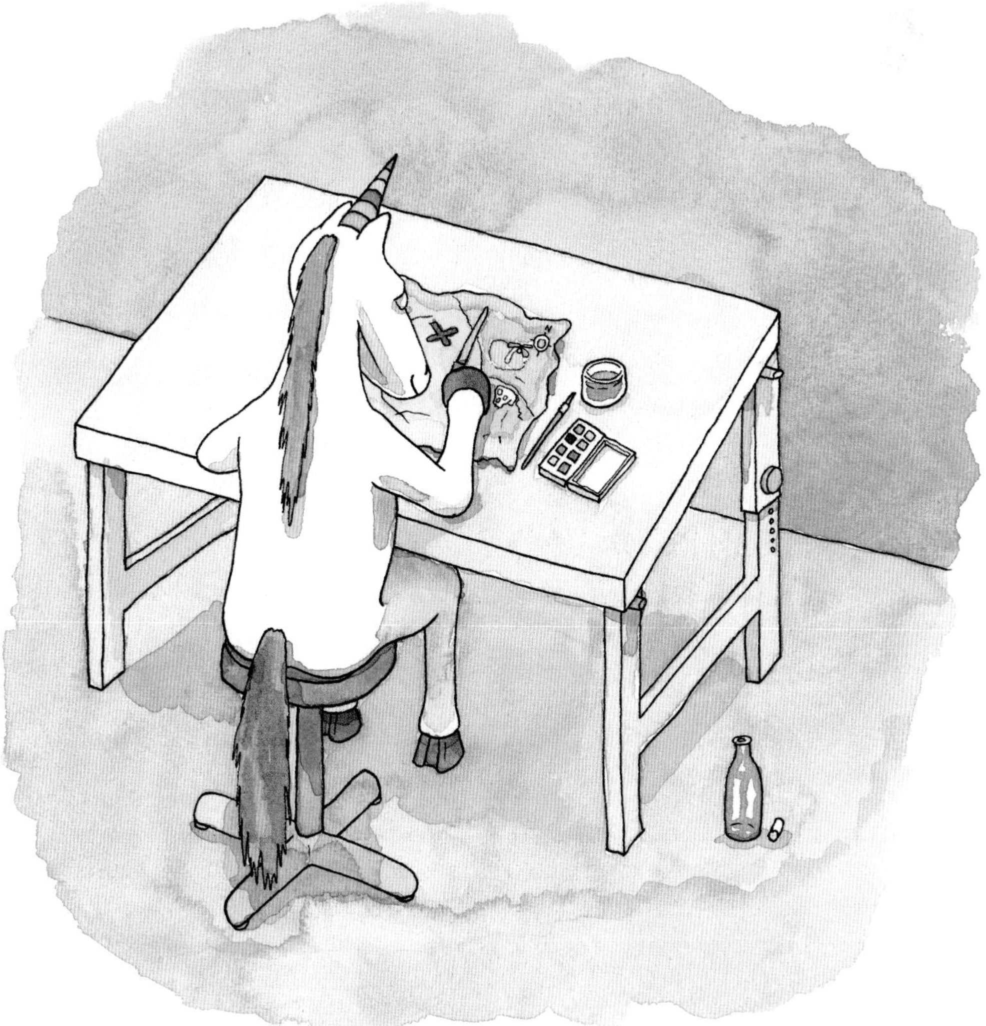

Freeing doves underneath a helicopter.

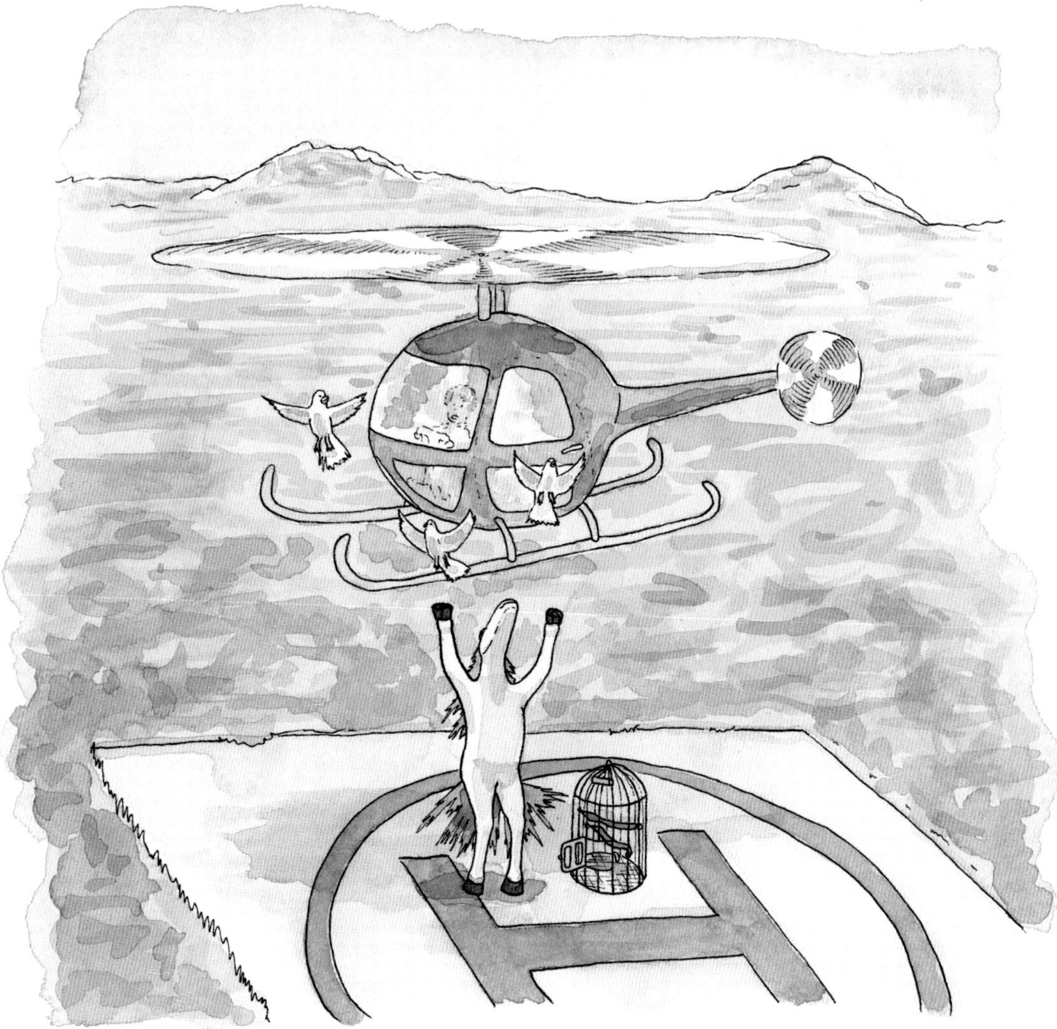

Wearing a t-shirt with himself on it.

Pointing out the illegal immigrants to the cops.

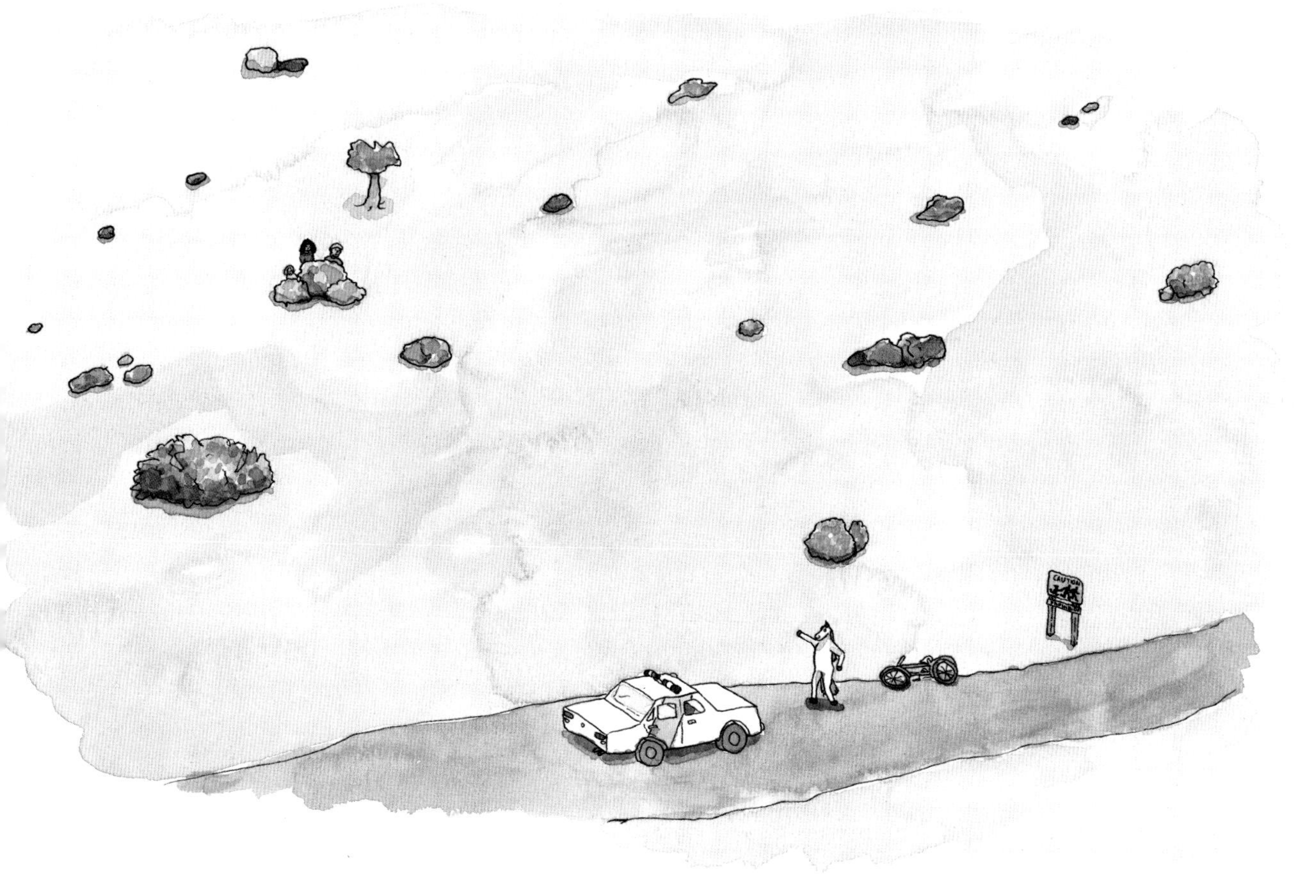
CAUTION

Making a Rube Goldberg machine to tickle the elderly.

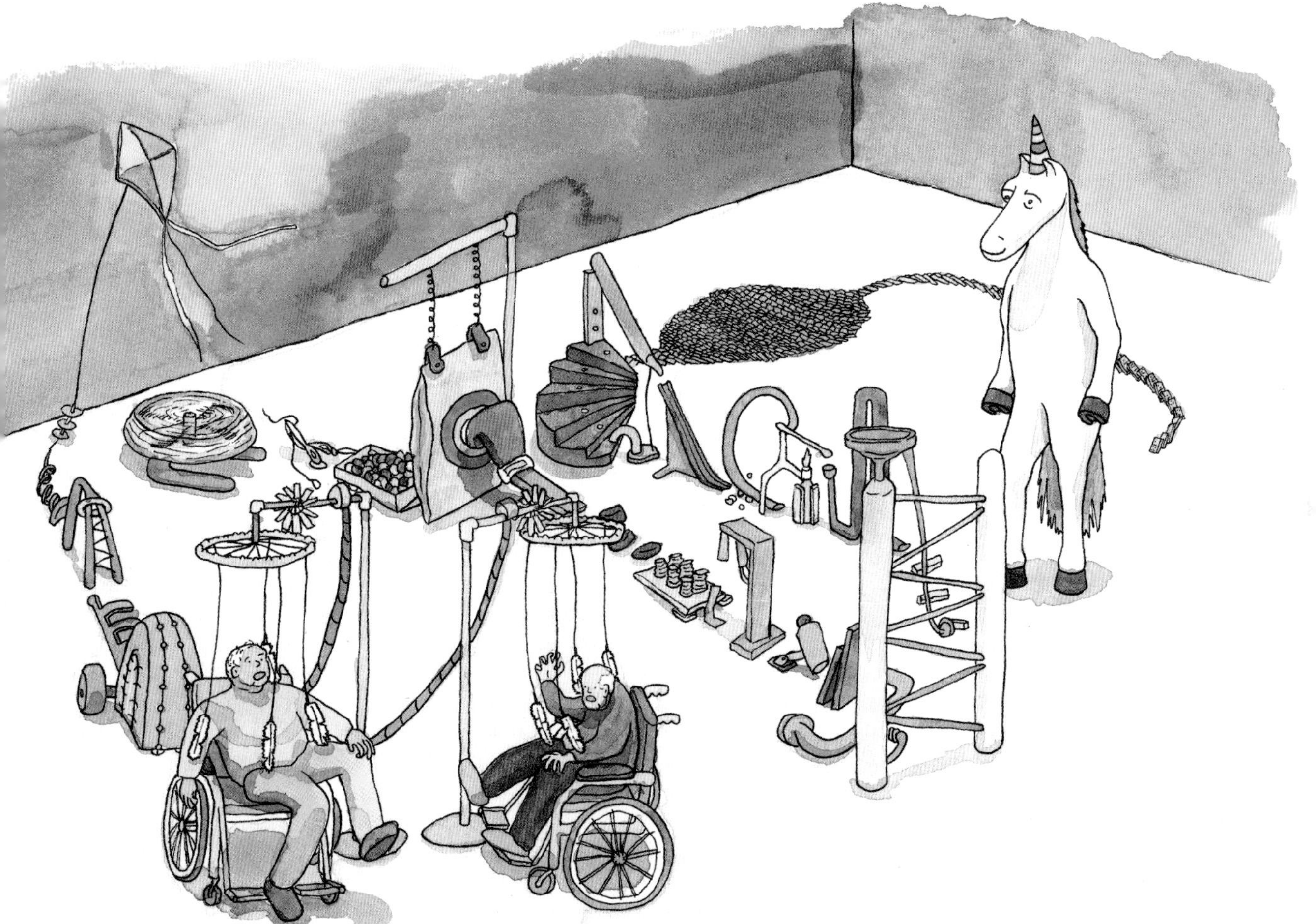

Agreeing with one political party completely and blindly.

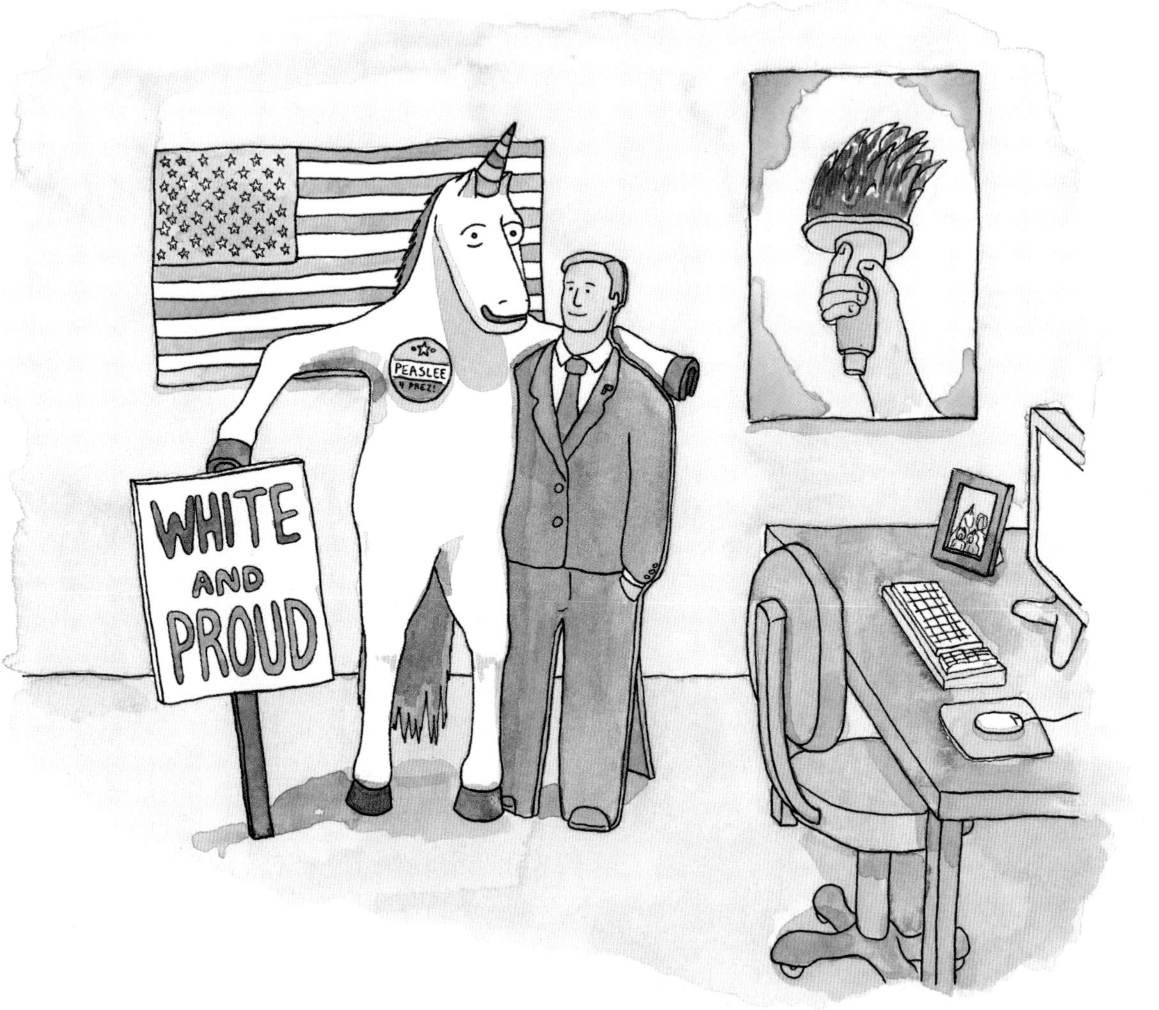
PEASLEE 4 PREZ!
WHITE AND PROUD

Upstaging the bride at her own wedding.

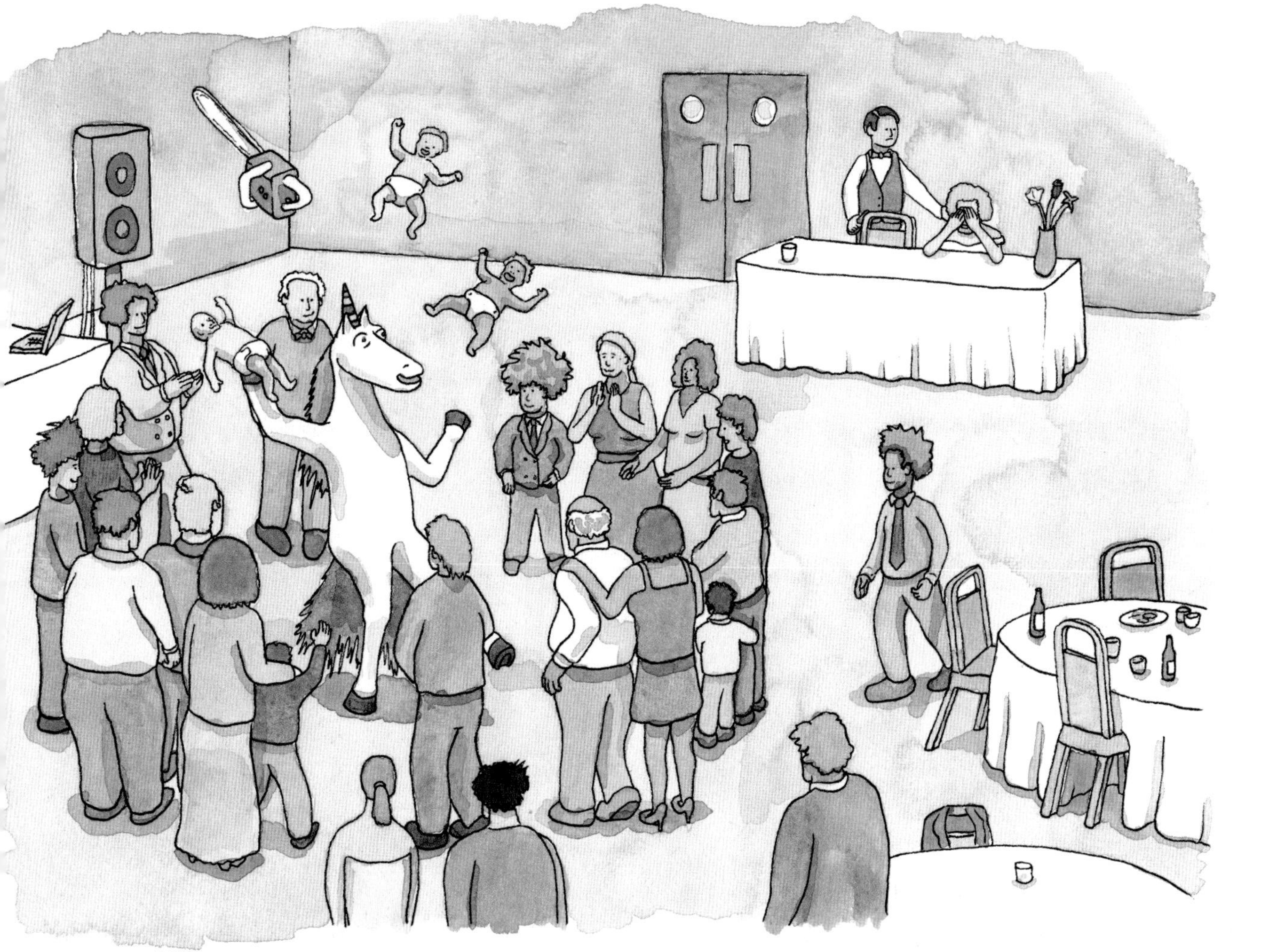

Stealing all the change from a fountain.

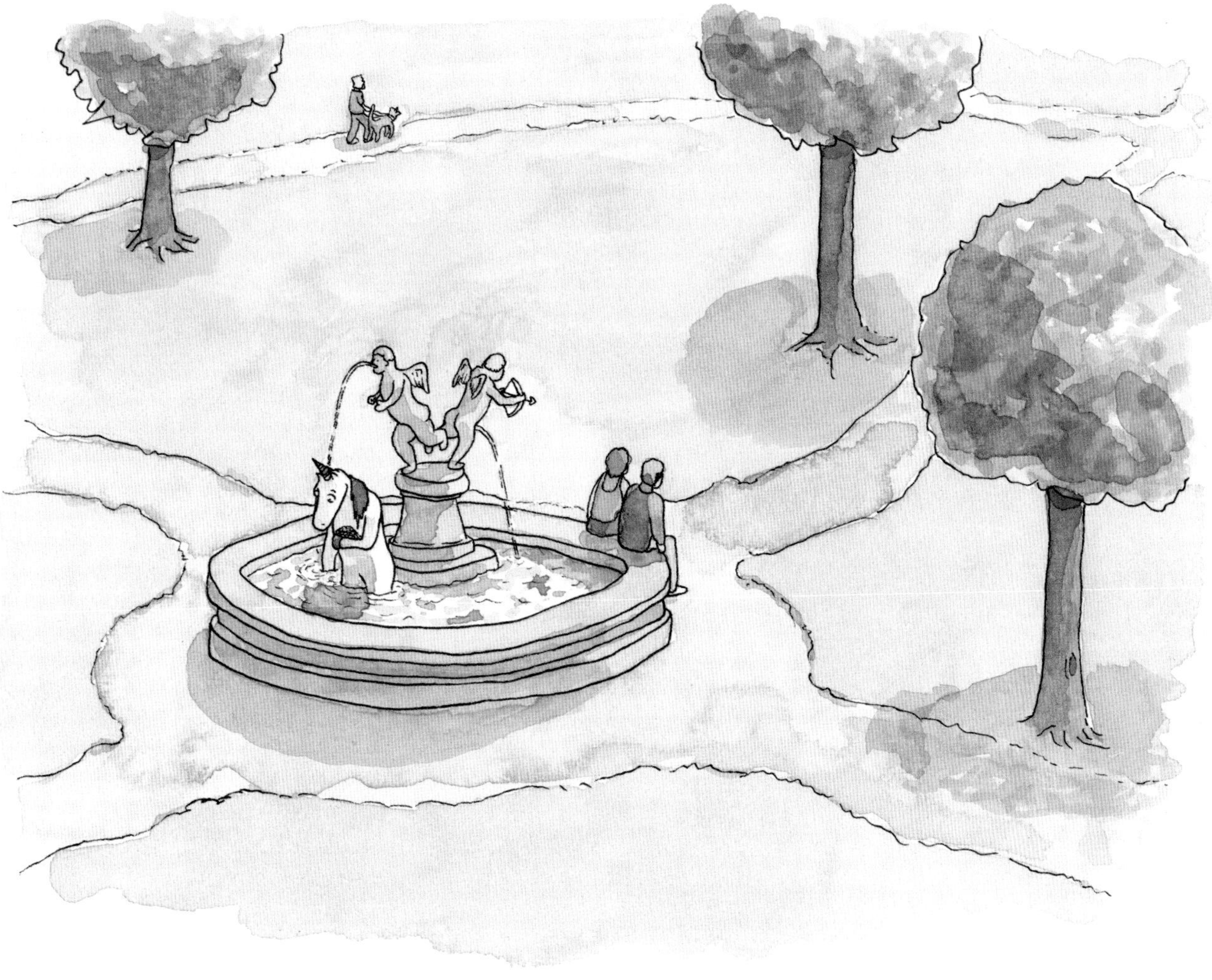

Paying with all change.

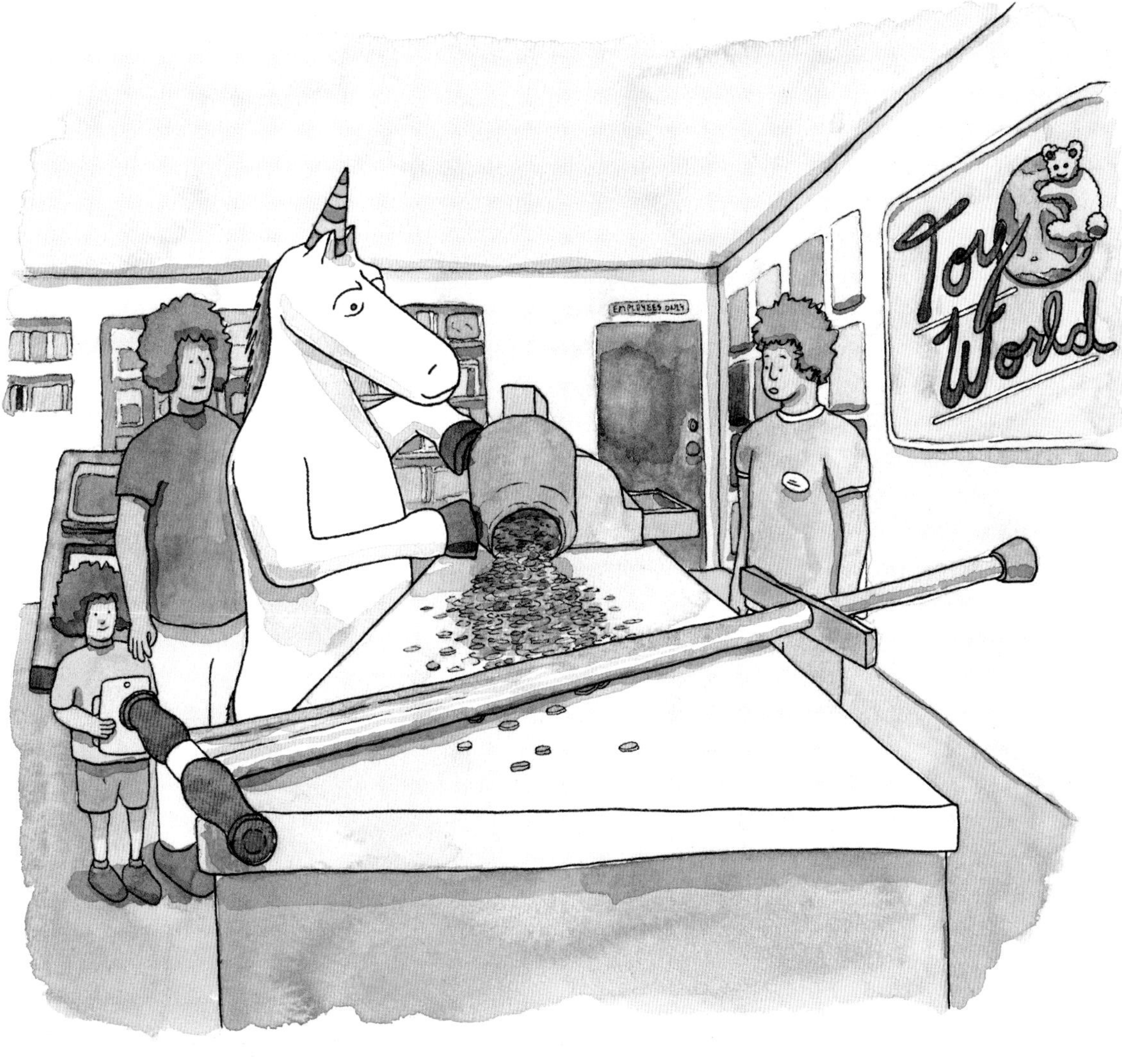
EMPLOYEES ONLY
Toy World

Getting into a fight at his son's little league game.

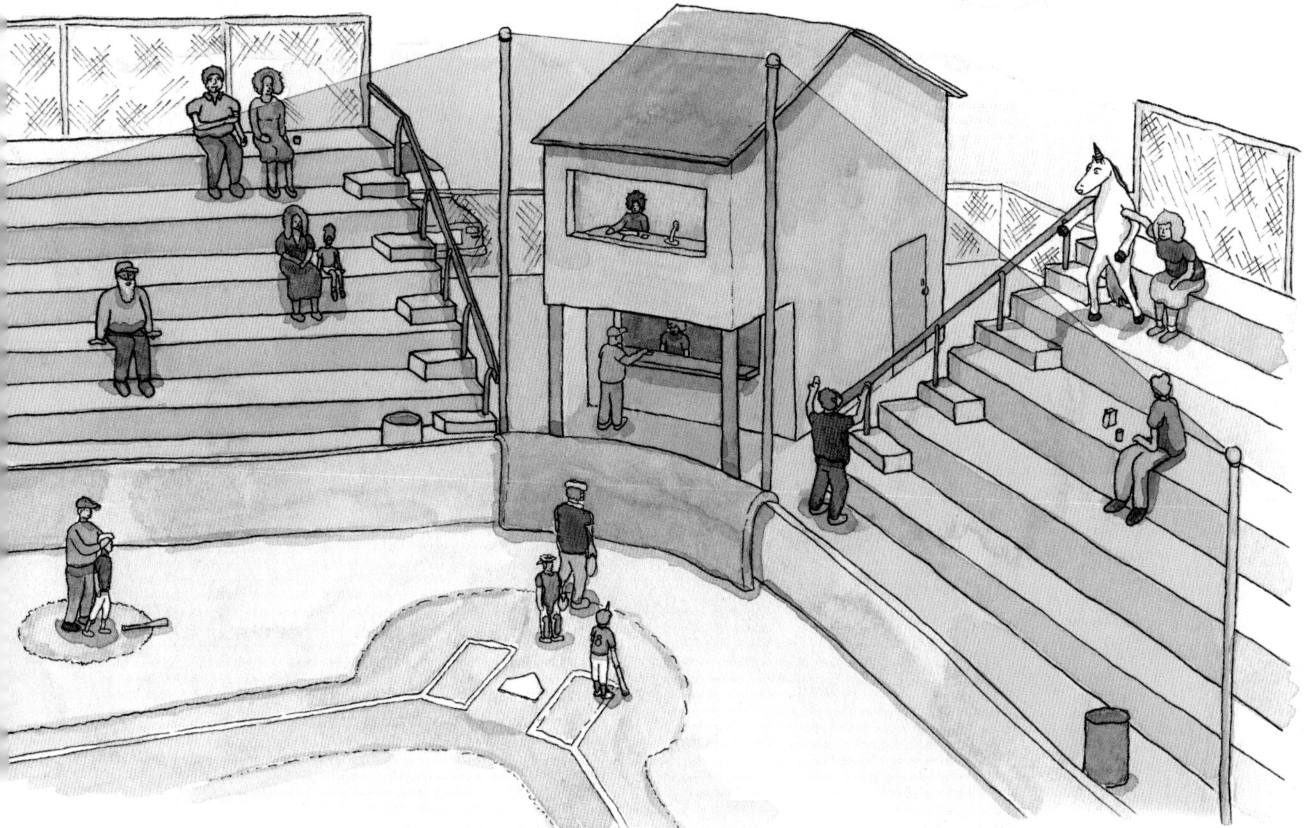

Still giving blood even though he has AIDS.

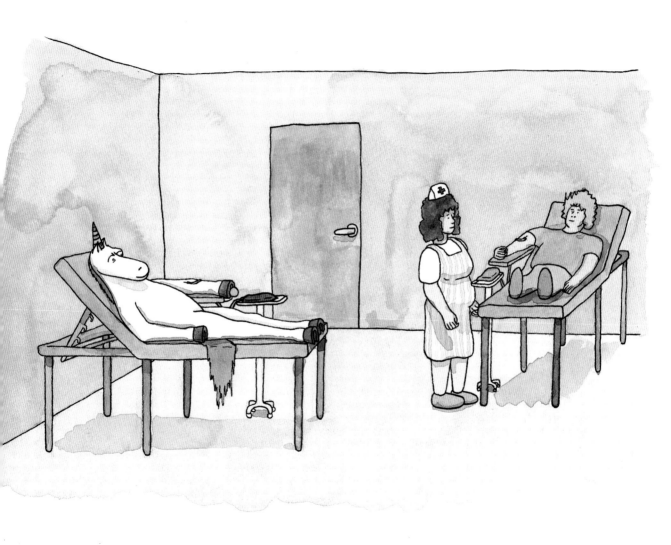

Supergluing his pubic hairs to the floor.

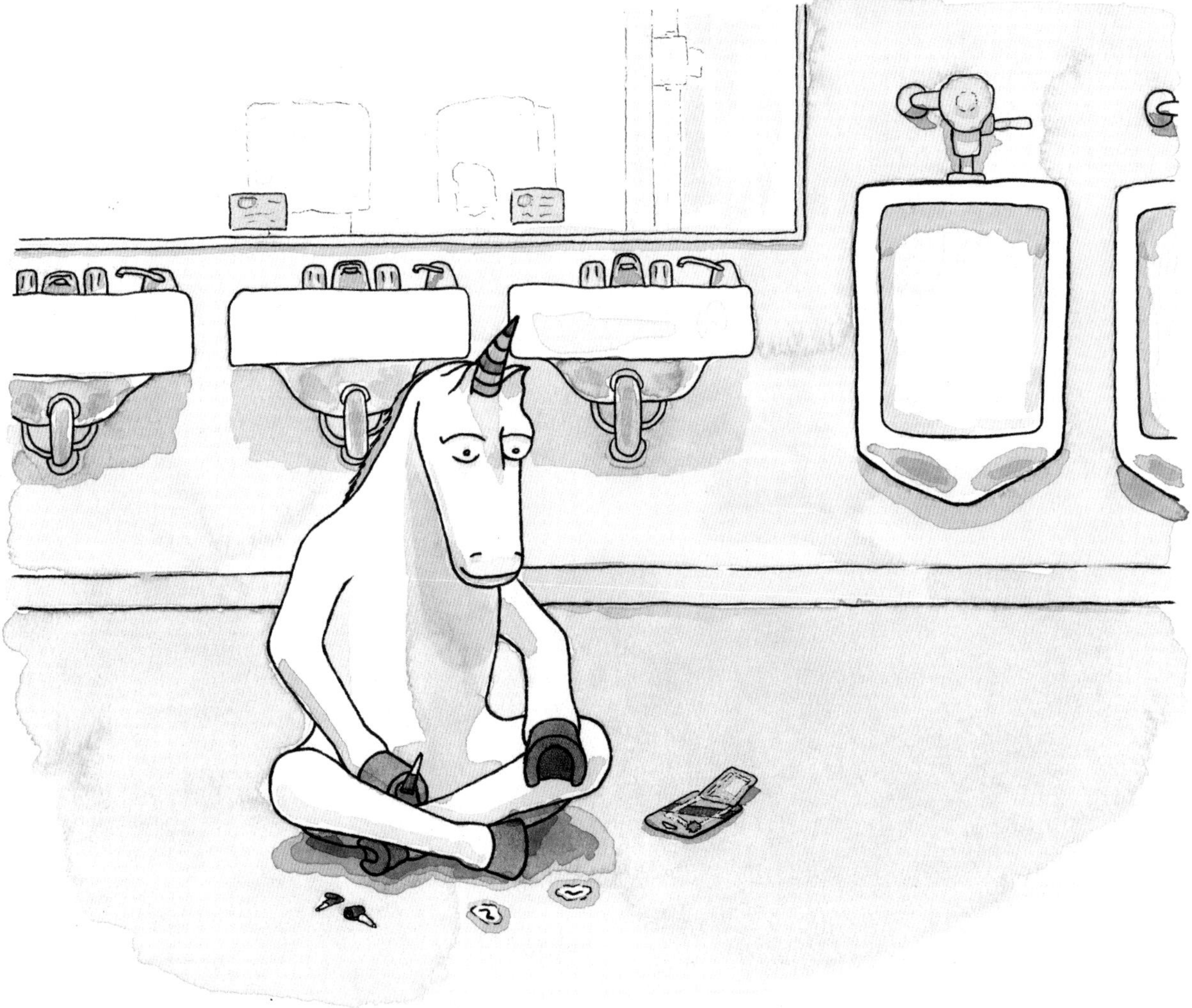

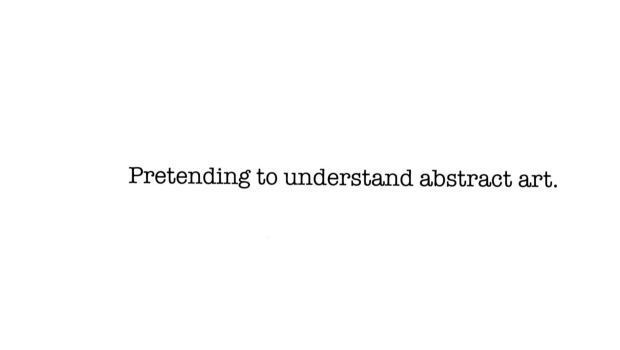

Pretending to understand abstract art.

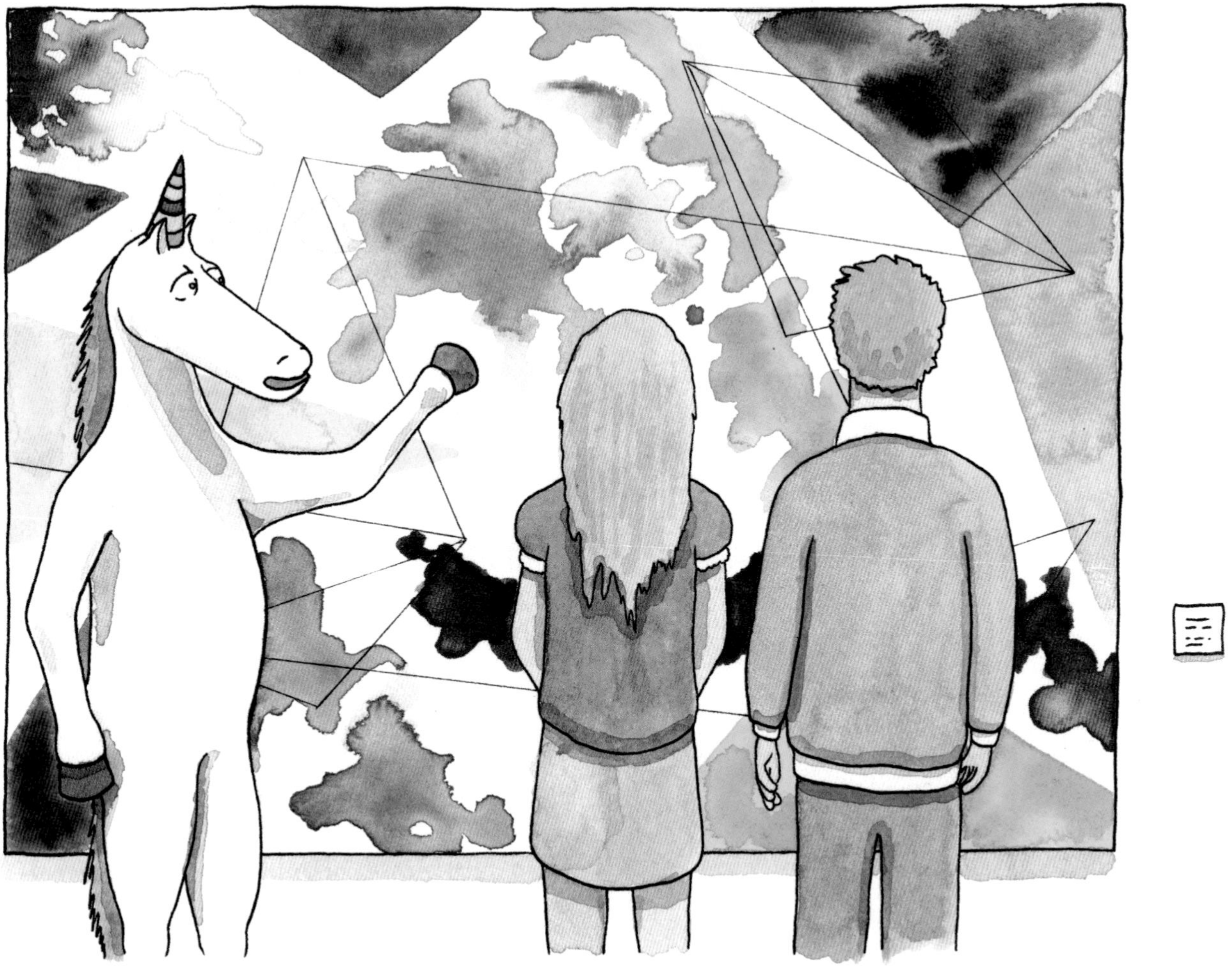

Smoking in the car with a pregnant woman.

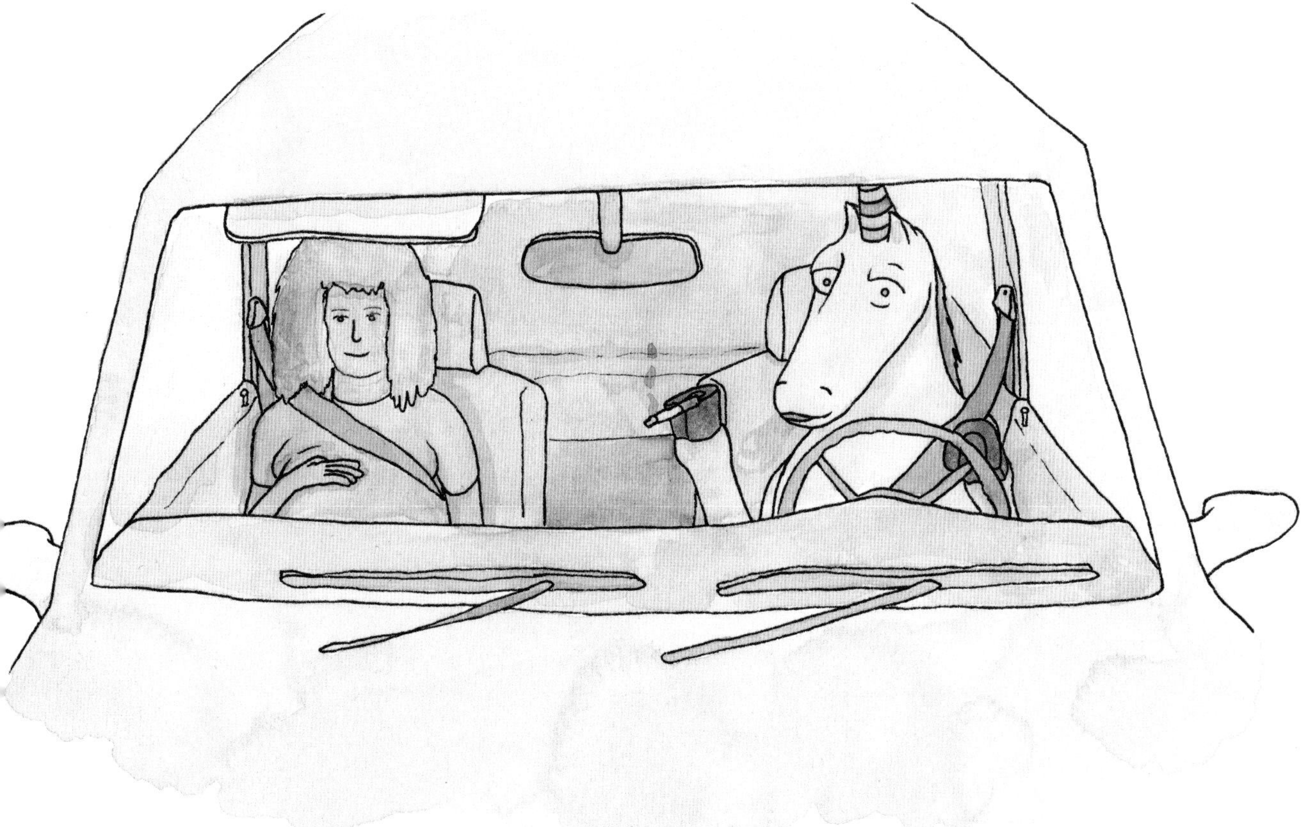

Buying plants to watch them die.

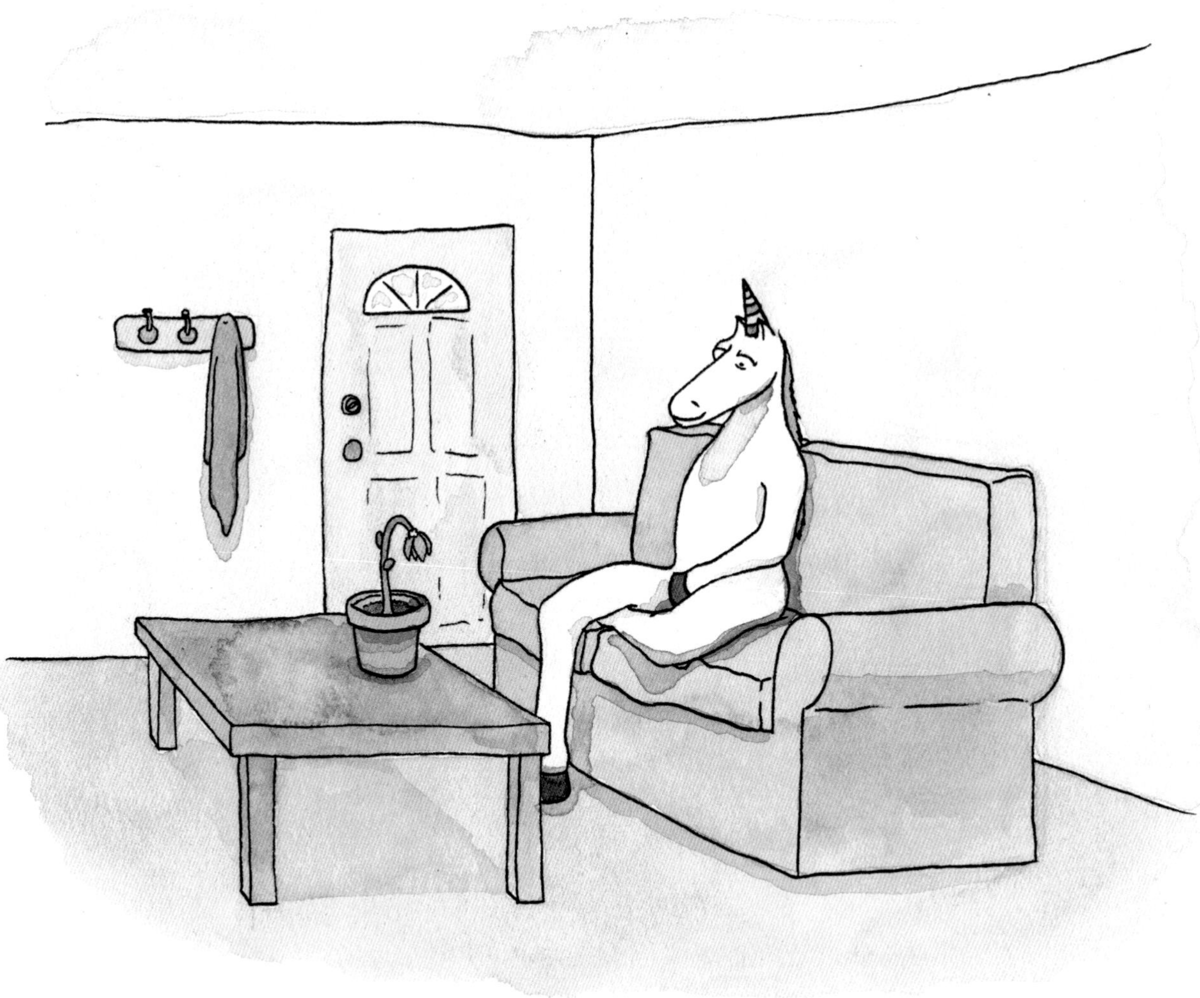

Painting his horn white to avoid the gay crowd.

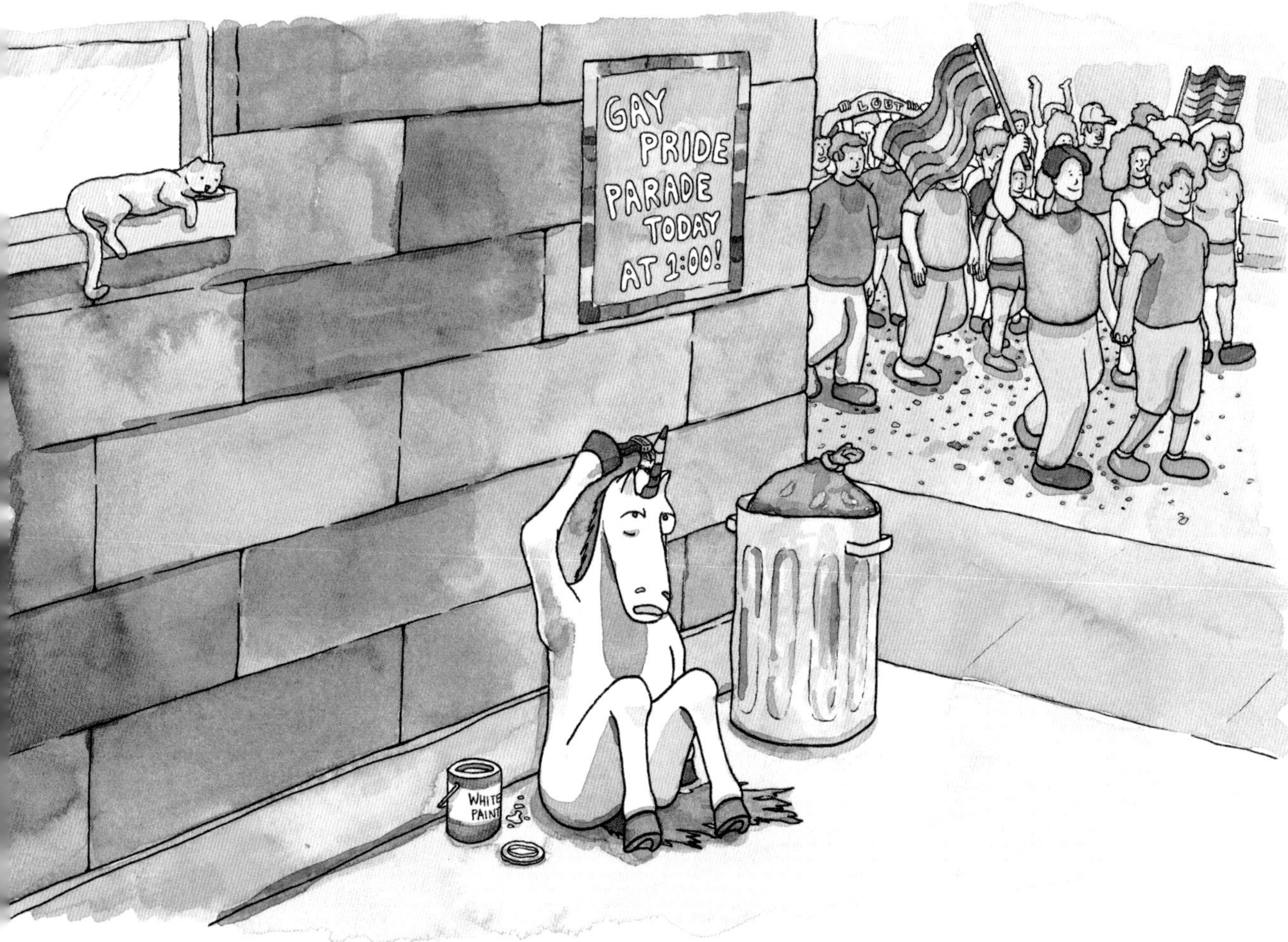
GAY PRIDE PARADE TODAY AT 1:00!
LGBT
WHITE PAINT

Ignoring the "10 items or less" sign.

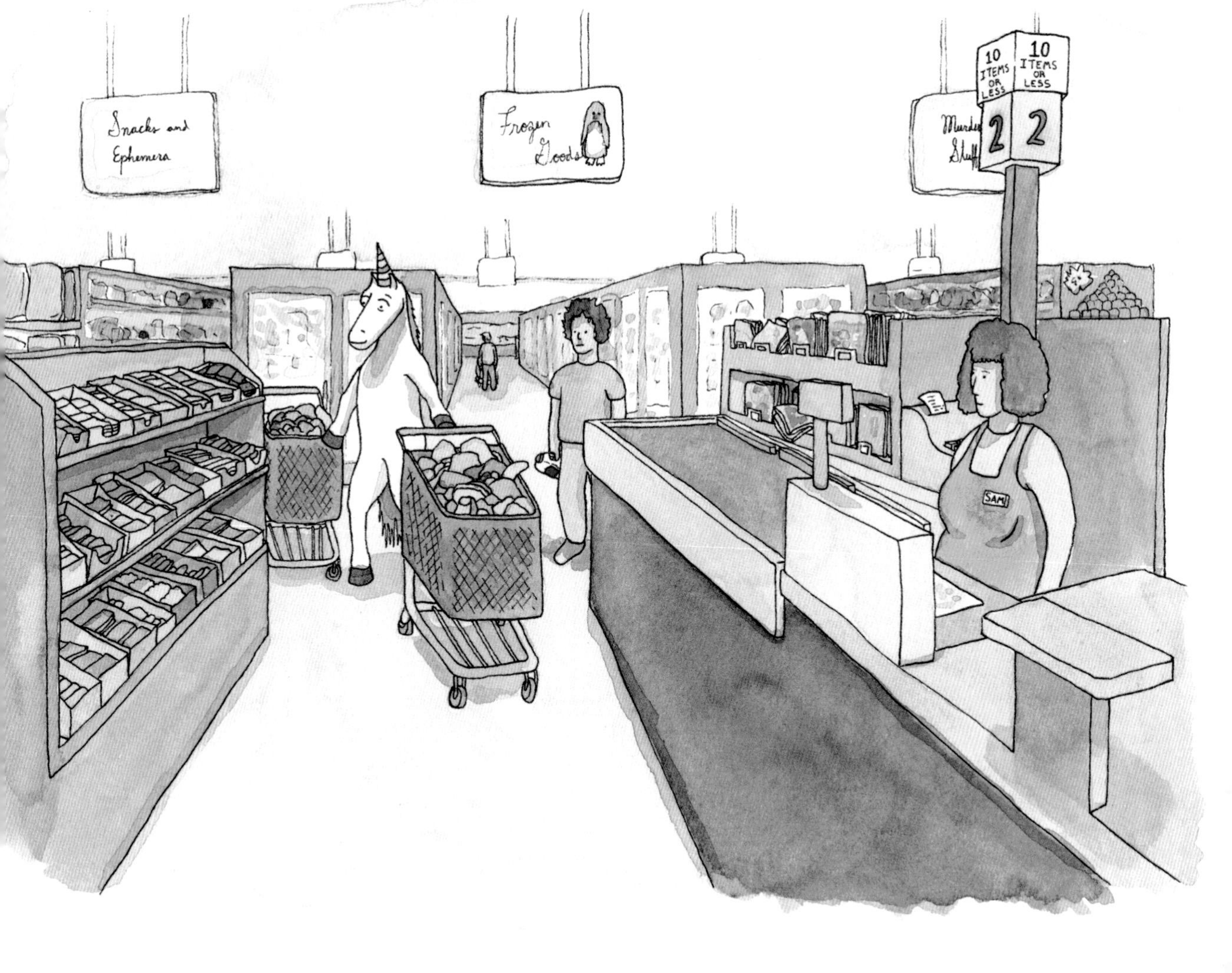
Snacks and Ephemera
Frozen Goods
10 ITEMS OR LESS
10 ITEMS OR LESS
2
2
SAM

Letting a baby play in a plastic bag.

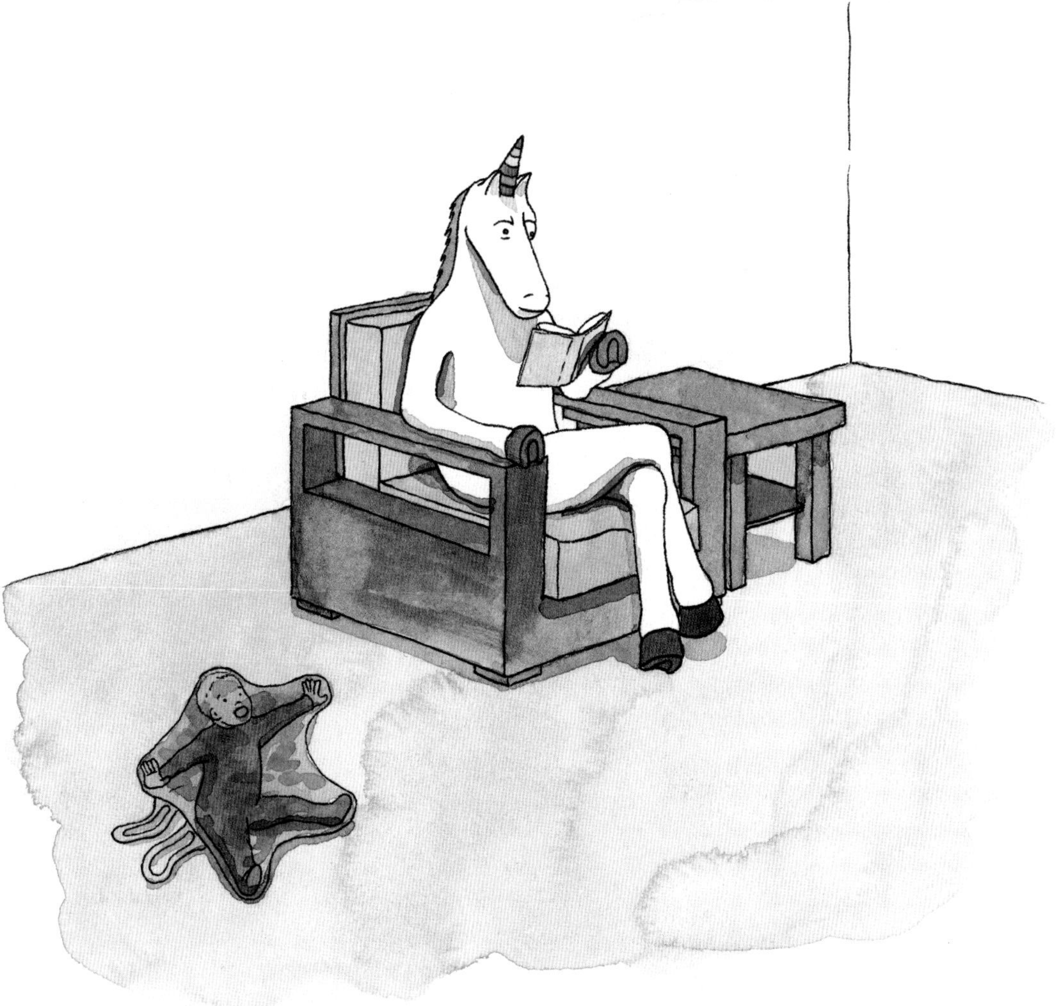

Putting his wiener on the water fountain.

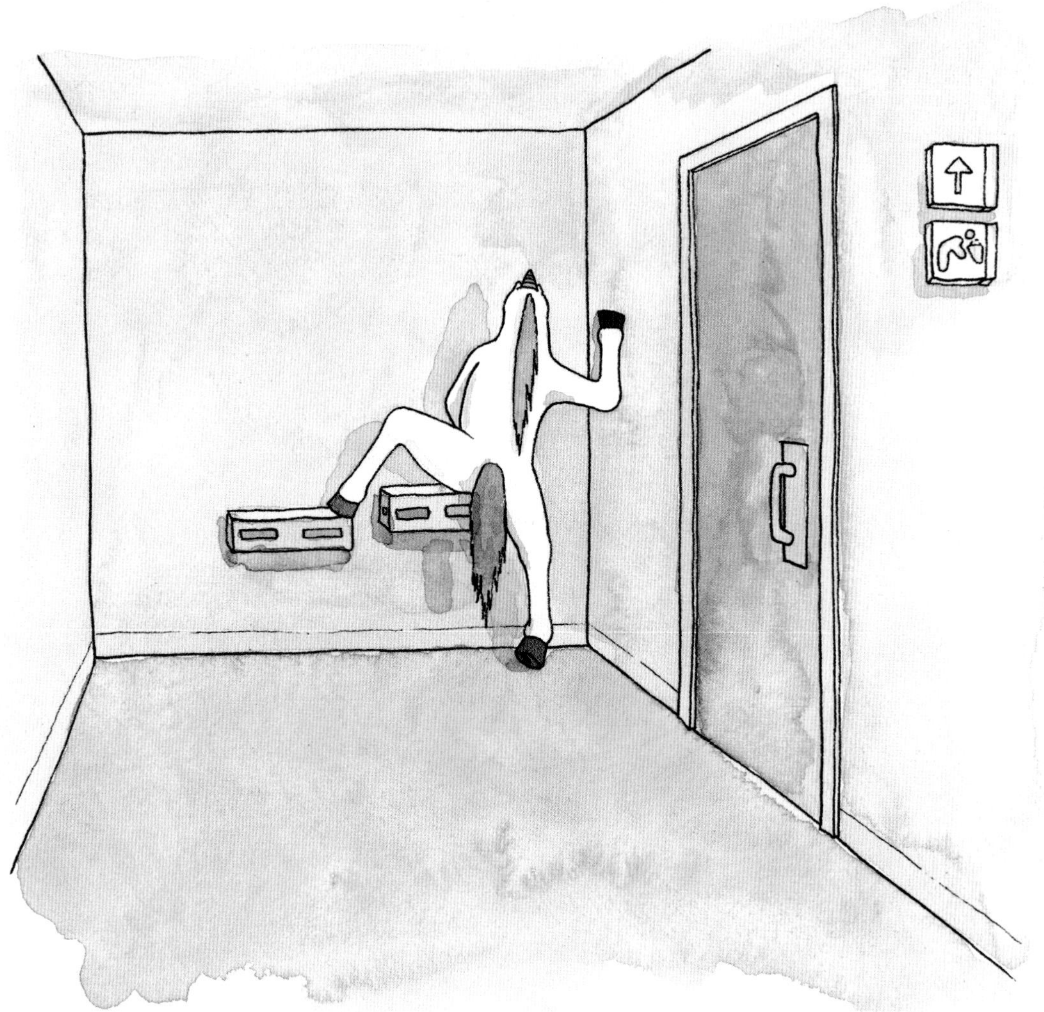

Eye-raping you.

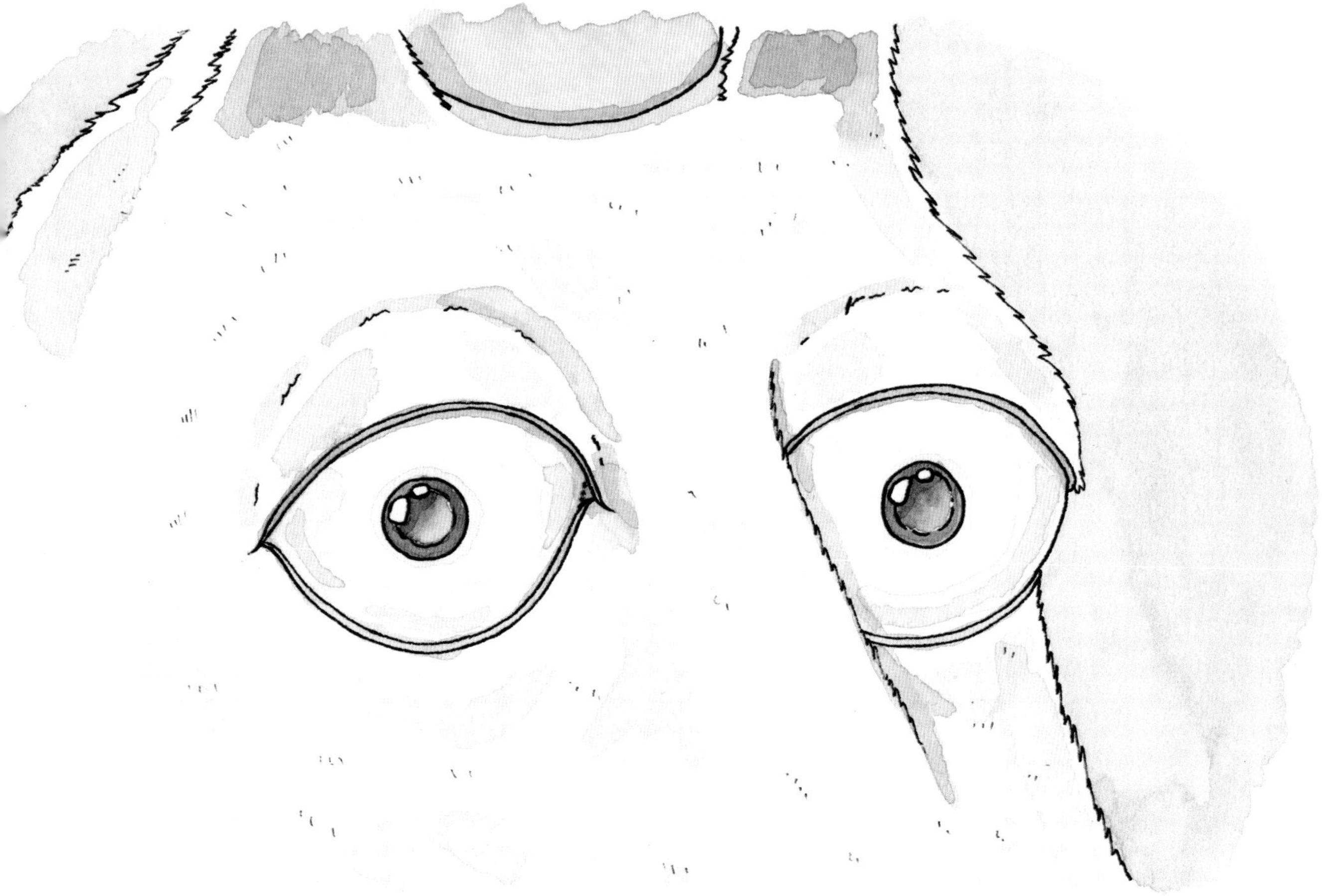

The end.

Thank you, Kate Hamill. Also, thank you: George,
John, Tiimo, Paul, Josh, Sam, Ashley, Lindsey,
Nicole, Jeff, Pat, Adam, Daniel, and Nathan.

*it*books

UNICORN BEING A JERK.

Copyright © 2011 by C.W. Moss. All rights reserved. Printed in China. No part of this book may be used or reproduced in any manner whatsoever without written permission except in the case of brief quotations embodied in critical articles and reviews. For information address HarperCollins Publishers, 10 East 53rd Street, New York, NY 10022.

HarperCollins books may be purchased for educational, business, or sales promotional use. For information please write: Special Markets Department, HarperCollins Publishers, 10 East 53rd Street, New York, NY 10022.

FIRST EDITION

Designed by C.W. Moss

Edited by Jennifer Schulkind

Library of Congress Cataloging-in-Publication Data is available upon request.

ISBN 978-0-06-207021-0

11   12   13   14   15   /RRD   10   9   8   7   6   5   4   3   2   1

Please, direct all questions, comments, and inquiries to:
jerk@misterunicorn.com

Find more on Unicorn at:
misterunicorn.com

Find more from C.W. Moss at:
greyrainbow.com